ST ROOSTER BOOKS

PRAISE FOR THE GOD PROVIDES!

"Tinker's Falls has a bogeyman, and Thomas R Clark is going to shock and fascinate you with this tale, woven so tightly and delivered so frankly right from the start, that you will cancel your calendar until you've read the last page! No author, thus far, has gripped me with touches of Celtic lore set in modern times the way Mr. Clark has." MIA MORAVIS, *Tony®-nominated Broadway Producer (JAGGED LITTLE PILL) & three-time Emmy® nominee*

"When you've been reading horror for over forty years, it's not often that you come across something new or surprising. The twist here was truly a surprise for this sometimes-jaded horror fan. Thomas R Clark is one of the few authors out there who can still do this for me!" PAMELA MORRIS, author of DARK HOLLOW ROAD

"This book is a very good re-imagining of the werewolf legends, as seen through a Celtic mythology lens. The storylines grab your attention and are told by a master storyteller. Highly recommended!" REV. ROBERT LEE "SKIP" ELLISON (ADF), author of THE SOLITARY DRUID

"Clark successfully weaves tales that incorporate myth, folklore, the supernatural, and alternative historical fiction involving the McEntire family and their closest kin. I did not want to put this down!" CHRISTINA RANGEL ELEANOR, THE VORACIOUS GNOME, Book Review Blog

"I feel like I'm at a campfire listening... I demand campfire

SOMETHING IS CURSED IN THE FOOTHILLS...

The wind cries and brings terror with it. Storm clouds and lightning carry the banshee wail, rolling on thunder past the crescent of the moon. The breath of summer blows from the south and west. It cascades across the rolling foothills, growing in power and intensity as it flows over the land.

The gusts assault the homesteads and farms settled throughout the region. They strike through the fields, picking up speed, racing across the flatlands of the valley. Dairy cattle shiver in panic within their stalls while the residents of the Foothills hide inside their beds. The howling gusts speak for their fear, invading their dreams, providing affirmation of the terrors of the night.

Abandon all hope, the voice of despair says to the inhabitants.

A patch of sunflowers, their heads bent in prayer, fight the wind and stand watch over a small clearing in an orchard, near a stretch of corn fields. From within, a flickering shines in the darkness. Inside walls of sunflower stalks, alone in her sanctuary, a woman fucks with ancient, cyclopean things she shouldn't.

THE GOD PROVIDES

ST ROOSTER BOOKS

stories by Thomas R Clark!" - LISA VASQUEZ, author of THE UNFLESHED

"You're not going to figure this out. You'll think you have more than once, but you'll be wrong. Clark is ahead of you every time. Enjoy." - JAY WILBURN, author of VAMPIRE CHRIST

"Literary perfection. Unique, evocative, flowing, and an excellent twist!" - LISA LEE TONE, Bibliophilia Templum

"Beginning with a series of gruesome murders, The God Provides spins the reader a grimly beautiful tale rooted in old world folklore and modern monster mythology." NIKOLAS P. ROBINSON, author of YOU WILL BE CONSUMED

"Werewolves are one of my favorite creatures to read about, and Clark delivers one hell of a werewolf tale in The God Provides. If you think you've read everything on lycanthrope lore, think again! This is the story of the Mac Tire family's twisted history, and comes complete with rich Irish lore, iconic characters, and the blood and gore to satisfy any horror fan. By the end of this book, you'll be chanting it too, because the author provides one hellish ride that you don't want to miss." - ERIN KELLY, Author of the TAINTED MOONLIGHT Series

"From a captivating opening to a thrilling ending, Tom Clark has crafted an engaging story that will keep you on edge months after you finish the final page." - JASON PITTS Writer/Director of THE FOREST TRHOUGH THE TREES

ST ROOSTER BOOKS

THOMAS R CLARK

THE GOD PROVIDES

ST ROOSTER BOOKS
ONEIDA, NY

ST ROOSTER BOOKS

For
Shawn Michael
and
Allison Bridie

ST ROOSTER BOOKS

CONTENTS

ST ROOSTER BOOKS

Samhain

Fireflies
and
Apple Pies

ST ROOSTER BOOKS

ST ROOSTER BOOKS

FIREFLIES AND APPLE PIES

When Mars shines in twilight skies,
And the hills howl at her might.
Will o' wisps chase fireflies
While spirits fill the night.

When shooting stars bake apple pies,
And all that's sown is reap'd.
Don't forget to close your eyes,
And pray your soul to keep.

Leatherstocking Bedtime Prayer

ST ROOSTER BOOKS

1

The bogeyman came early to the Tully Foothills the year they canceled Halloween. It arrived with the first frost, before the leaves transformed into shades of fire, culling those foolish enough to wander after sundown. In fear for their lives, the good residents locked their doors at night. They huddled within the safety of their homes and waited for the last harvest to come.

For decades, the annual Apple Festival graced the foothills the first weekend in October. The event hammered the final nail into summer's coffin, ushering in fall. Visitors came from across upstate New York to attend the event, pouring money into the local economy.

Tents full of crafters and vendors selling country wares covered the hillsides. Hordes waited patiently in long lines for apple fritters and fried dough. Carnival foods filled the air with their delicious aromas. A festive midway with a variety of rides, including a giant Ferris Wheel, lit up the night with fluorescent lights.

The clean-up crew discovered Sandy Gillman's body behind a dumpster. The bogeyman expressed a penchant for the extravagant, leaving Ms. Gillman sitting up and smiling. At first, it appeared as though preschoolers went to town practicing covering her mouth with lipstick.

"She looked like she stuck her face in a can of strawberry jam." One of the workers told a TV reporter.

But no.

A closer examination revealed someone ripped out Sandy's tongue and left her to bleed to death, alone in the dark. The girl graduated a year ago and, like many locals, she worked at the festival to make a few extra bucks. The day before her smiling face could be seen at a Fritter booth. Now no one could find her tongue.

The State Troopers labeled the foothill's first murder in a century an anomaly. Security cameras and witnesses didn't help identify the culprit. Detectives focused on suspects from Syracuse, or further away, who came in for the festival.

They stopped blaming city folk the following week.

Steve Rouse, the Pompey Tigers Pee Wee Football coach arrived early at the field on Saturday morning. He found Betsy Van Bramer gutted and presented for display, spread-eagle, in the home team's endzone. Betsy's internal organs sat in a neat stack next to her eyeless head. He stared at the black voids on the woman's face for ten minutes, until nausea overtook him.

After vomiting, Steve made two phone calls: the first to 911 to report the incident. The second to his assistant to keep the kids away from the scene.

Rouse sat in his van and stayed there until the troopers arrived. The State Police detectives stared in disbelief at the vulgar display of carnography. Rouse took advantage of the distraction and secured a shotgun from one of the cruisers.

"No one should ever witness something like this," he announced and blew his head off before a trooper could stop him.

Naturally, detectives believed they might have their double murderer, albeit posthumously. The State Police detectives searched Rouse's home for any evidence connecting him to the mutilations, things like tongues or eyeballs. Investigators found nothing of the sort, but they continued to look. This lasted a whole three days until Joanne Mitchell's body turned up.

Crucified to an apple tree, her face peeled off and pinned onto her belly with her finger bones.

The killer once again took the victim's eyes as a trophy. Joanne's fresh body eliminated Steve Rouse as suspect zero.

Realizing a predatory serial killer chose their home as its feeding ground for whatever reason, authorities established a curfew. This effectively closed down trick-or-treating, making the tradition one more victim of the murderer.

One can always count on a creative journalist to come up with a clever moniker for any bogeyman. The media came through on this promise and dubbed their new darling *The Foothills Slasher*.

"She looked like she stuck her face in a can of strawberry jam."

ST ROOSTER BOOKS

2

None of this stopped Rose McEntire from going home. She made the trip every year without fail since moving to the city. A career in the fashion industry seduced her away from the foothills, but Rose refused to let it contain her. She couldn't imagine being any place other than home for the last harvest.

Rose missed her mother's smile and her father's stoicism. The yearning grew for the earthen aroma of cinnamon and apples baked together, the crisp scent of dead leaves crunching under her boot, and how it all permeated her curly mop of long, black hair.

Smiling, she thought of a home-cooked meal, made with local vegetables and regional meat, and goddamn Byrne Dairy chocolate milk. Crocheting with her sister Erin, sipping hot cocoa after dinner on the porch, and racing her through the apple orchards were on the agenda. Most of all? Rose yearned for the last harvest, and the feast to follow.

Memories of the aroma of a dining room table decked out in a smorgasbord of country-cooked goodies came to mind. Everything from pies to baked squash, venison steaks, and roasted turkey. Nothing would, or could, stop her from going home for this. Especially not the bogeyman.

The youngest McEntire packed a bag and hopped on a Greyhound like she did so many times before. Rose reminisced for five hours, as the bus snaked through the country highways of upstate New York. The tires and engine hummed, creating a soothing, ambient drone until the bus reached her destination: the hamlet of Tinker's Falls.

3

Typically, the shadow of Morgan Hill, the region's tallest peak, brought dusk a bit earlier to the Tully Foothills. Tonight, however, steady rain and clouds obscured the sun. Premature darkness engulfed Tinker's Falls as the Greyhound arrived at its destination. The bus stop's primary role as a Byrne Dairy convenience store and gas station became apparent. The front door hissed open, and Rose McEntire stepped off the bus, onto the parking lot.

The rain bit into her face, forcing her to run for cover under the fluorescent lights of the convenience store. Rose looked at the time on her phone and wondered where her ride might be. She saw a tall woman with blue highlights streaked through her long blonde hair. Deep blue eyeshadow offset her smokey, hazel eyes. At first Rose didn't recognize her. Then, as she stepped out of the building, a refreshing wave filled her with glee.

The woman, Rose's sister, dressed in *basic bitch* attire, including a puffy vest and calf-high leather boots. Gaudy hoop earrings slapped against her neck, and enough gold chains to encircle the county at least once hung from her neck. She stepped out of the sliding doors of the store with a grocery bag in hand.

"Took you long enough, didn't it?" Erin said, "I don't know who to blame, you or the bus. Use an Uber next year. It'll bring you to the house, among other things."

"So good to see you, too, Erin. When did you add the special K to your name?" Rose taunted her elder sibling. The tall blonde stood out as Rose's photo-negative in both her appearance and demeanor. By contrast, Rose wore blue jeans, a Superman T-shirt, sneakers, and a black hoodie. A silver pentacle, hanging off a leather thong around her neck, amounted to the extent of Rose's jewelry.

"Hah hah! Very funny. The fucking clerk in there is terrified she's going to get murdered by the Foothills Slasher tonight. I almost hopped over the counter, poked her eyes out, and obliged. For fuck's sake, this place needs a makeover. Fucking inbred hicks. I've seen two Confederate flags this month. That's two, too many! How the fuck can they forget?"

"Dad would remind you those hicks buy apples from us, and Mom would crack jokes about everything that will rise before the south ever does. And one more thing," She flipped Erin her middle finger. "An Uber would cost three hundred bucks. I have better things to spend my money on." Erin repaid the gesture with a finger of her own.

"Oh, I'm sorry. Not really," the blonde woman rolled her eyes, "Oh, come on! Is that any way to treat someone who brings you chocolate milk?" Erin held up a half-gallon glass bottle of Byrne Dairy milk. Their playful, sarcastic banter typically deceived onlookers.

"You do know the way to get on my good side," Rose shook her head and smiled. She truly loved her sister.

"And I always will, little sister." She motioned to a cobalt blue Kia SUV parked next to the bus. The bay lights of the canopy glowed off its reflective paint.

"The blue streaks in your hair threw me off."

"I put them in for the Last Harvest. They're perfect don't you think?" Erin said. Rose nodded in affirmation.

"Come on, get in, let's get home, so we can eat and you can meet my fiancé."

"Pardon me. What did you say?" Rose stopped moving, not believing she heard her sister right.

Did she just say 'fiancé'? Rose thought. Over the

years Erin built a reputation for shocking people. The hair, now this. Tonight, her sister delivered the hits like she joined the Beatles. They kept coming … and coming.

"Chad Gowing, my fiancé."

She fucking did say 'fiancé'! Rose answered internally, then added, verbally, "Excuse me, but why is this news to me?" She cocked her head and squinted at her sister.

"Don't you give me that look. I met him in a MyFace group, and invited him down for the Apple Festival, and, well, things kind of took off, and here we are. I swear I was at the festival the night they found the dead Gillman girl. If Chad hadn't been with me, I could've been the first victim." Rose couldn't believe her ears. She spoke with Erin almost daily. Her sister never once mentioned a fiancé, let alone dating any men or any close encounter with a serial killer. "I made Mom and Dad swear not to tell you. I wanted to surprise you. He's so fucking cool. He's a musician and a writer. And he's so fucking romantic."

"I bet he is," Rose said, "and Dad approves of this?"

"Who cares what Dad says. Come on, get in the car. We have to be home before curfew in ten minutes. I don't want to have to deal with any troopers tonight." Rose got in the SUV with Erin, and the siblings drove off to their home. They traveled in silence, remaining ever vigilant for anything lurking in the night. Both sisters feared the random deer crossing the highway more than any bogeyman. All along, Rose's mind couldn't help but wonder.

Why would my sister lie to me about a boy?

4

Tiffani Mason knew she shouldn't be out walking so close to curfew, but she needed a pack of cigarettes. The Byrne Dairy stood close enough, a fifteen-minute walk in one direction. This gave her half an hour plus a fifteen-minute cushion. It cut it close, but it also allowed the addiction to overcome her fear.

Getting there, strolling down a slight incline, proved to be an easy feat. After procuring her smokes and bottle of diet Pepsi, the return trip proved to be a different challenge. Moving uphill, Tiff found herself slowing down and running out of breath with each step. It slowed her down, and darkness came far too early.

Halfway home she stopped to rest, and an ice-cold rain, complete with gigantic droplets, started falling. She shook her head.

"Son of a bitch," she said, took a drag from her cigarette, and kicked an errant rock sitting on the shoulder of State Route 11. It skipped across the road and disappeared into the ditch. The rain pierced the cotton of her hoodie. She pulled the hood up. Her face and fingers felt the bite of the cold. She let the cigarette hang from her lip and stuffed her hands into the kangaroo pocket of her sweatshirt.

The high beams of a subcompact sedan lit up the night, momentarily blinding the woman, walking against the traffic. As it drew closer, Tiffani could make out the Toyota logo. The car blew by at fifty-five, spraying her with rain in its wake. The water extinguished her cigarette and soaked the paper, ruining it. Tiff spit it out and pushed on to her home, pissed off and regretting ever going out.

"Fuck you! Drive American! You're prolly a libtard commie!" Tiff shot her arm in the air, and without looking back, she flipped the car the bird.

A burst of lightning followed by a booming crack of thunder startled her. She picked up the pace as the rain continued to fall harder and heavier. She swore off cigarettes, nothing justified walking in this shit.

Something plowed into her, throwing her body into the air. As she tumbled, she wondered if the libtards in the Japanese car got pissed and decided to kill her. Her mind entertained the thought until she landed on the road's shoulder.

The impact slammed her head on the blacktop,

face first, knocking her out. The blow crushed her nose, shattered her jaw, and split her skull open. Her unconscious body bounced off the road and rolled into the ditch. She left behind a bloody splotch riddled with teeth.

Tiffani woke to a throbbing pain in her face. Bolts of liquid ice pierced her flesh, adding to the agony. She wanted to scream, but her mouth wouldn't work. Instead, a garbled, unintelligible mumble fell off numb lips. She decided getting up would be the best course of action.

She couldn't move.

Am I paralyzed? Tiffani pondered. Panic now overtook the woman. None of her limbs would respond.

No ... no ... no!

Tiff's head tipped to the side, giving her a view of the embankment, she tumbled down. She saw the ambient lights of LaFayette, Tully, and Tinker's Falls on the horizon.

A black and lightless automobile rolled to a stop, off the shoulder of the road. A door opened, a shadowed figure exited the vehicle and walked down the embankment. They walked with slow determination. Tiffani couldn't see her murderer, but she knew their identity.

The Foothills Slasher chose her this night.

My dumb luck!

The Slasher tied a rope to each of Tiffani's wrists

and hoisted her into the air. Fiery torment burned in her shoulders, pulling the bones out of their sockets. Unable to articulate words, she could still scream. The noise she brought forth resembled a soured brass section in a broken marching band. The wail of a wounded beast.

Her legs joined her outstretched arms, tied at the ankles, and hyperextended. A chilling cold covered her body when the torturer ripped Tiff's clothing off. The rain washed her clean.

She remembered the kinky guy she met at the horror convention a few years before. He tied Tiffani up, too, and she liked it. He used a safe word, though, if things went too far.

What was it?

Did the Foothills Slasher use a magic word to end the misery? If one existed, she doubted the Slasher would be giving it up, and Tiffani couldn't speak to ask what it may be. The thought became moot when she saw the knife in her assailant's gloved hand.

Wonder ... wonder what?

The blade pierced her left optical socket first, electrifying pain filled her head. Tiffani's constant wailing raised in pitch. The Slasher twisted the blade, scooping her eyeball out with a popping sound.

Tiff's wail became a boiling tea kettle.

Wonder ...

Tiffani Mason thought she blacked out when she no longer could feel the sensation of the blade slipping behind her right eye.

... wall!

Then the first blow to her back struck, slicing through the flesh into the bone, telling her unconsciousness would not bless her and dull the pain.

In the throes of utter agony, her mouth somehow articulated a single word.

"Wonderwall!" Tiffani managed to scream out. By responding with another strike, cutting into the ribs bordering the woman's spine, the slasher confirmed her suspicions.

Clearly, serial killers didn't give a fuck about safe words, Tiffani noted. She assumed more could be said about the glee they shared in hacking a person apart.

The agony remained constant, and she could feel the pressure of each blow the Slasher chopped into her back. As she pondered what she did to deserve this fate, Tiffani Mason aspirated and fell into eternity's abyss.

The rain increased in volume and washed away the imprint of Tiffani's faceplant. The trees lining the hills along State Route 11 drank their fill and listened to flesh sing as it ripped from cartilage, sinew, and bone.

5

The McEntire homestead was off State Route 11, three-quarters of a mile down Spruce Pond Road. A big slate-blue raised ranch, it rested on the edge of Mac Tire's apple orchards and fields. A large barn, which doubled as a tractor garage and apple warehouse, sat behind the house.

A pair of jack o' lanterns guarded the property. Carved into conical, pumpkin-sized yellow turnips, the sentinels greeted the McEntire's guests. Candles flickered away inside the neeps. The light filtered through the raindrops, creating twisted and distorted shapes on the lawn.

Standing under the cover of the porch of their farmhouse, Peggy and Jack McEntire greeted their daughter. Rose hugged her mother and kissed her father on the cheek. The pouring rain matched Jack McEntire's cranky disposition, and he scowled, warding off any intended hugs from his daughter. Instead, they settled for Stoic nods.

"It's about time. It's late, we shouldn't be out gallivanting around after dark," her father scorned.

"Jack, your daughter misses you. Come on, dinner is waiting on the table," Peggy interjected.

The McEntire patriarch nodded in approval and the group retired to the dining room. In the adjoining family room, a blue/green tartan blanket covered the sofa and Celtic-knot art adorned the walls. Above and around the fireplace hung a menagerie of archaic weapons. A pair of swords, a giant Scottish claymore, and an officer's saber paralleled one another. Matching musket pistols sat on pegs next to a liberated Brown Bess musket and crossed Iroquois tomahawks with polished, cast iron heads. An 1872 Winchester repeating rifle complimented the musket.

"Hola, Rosie," Rory Brannigan, the family's migrant worker foreman, waved to her. A thick white beard covered his wrinkled face. The old man always smiled; a trait Rose grew to appreciate through the years.

The McEntires always hired migrant workers to pick the harvest apples; it allowed them to maintain affordable prices for the lower-income families in the foothills. Now, with the season-ending, the crew returned to their homeland, leaving Uncle Rory, a local, to care for the property in the off-season.

Peggy busied about, ensuring the last bits of the meal were to her satisfaction. Turkey, with giblet gravy, corn, mashed taters, and sausage sage stuffing. Plenty of carbs to fuel an active family.

A pair of headlights lit up the driveway and shone through the picture window. Erin hopped up, a giant grin on her face.

"It's Chad!" She said and ran out to the door. Rose saw the joy in her sister's face and conceded she must like him. This didn't obligate Rose to pre-approve anyone. Chad would have to prove himself to her.

Jesus Christ on a broken fucking crutch, who calls their child Chad? What a dick name, she shook her head, keeping the thought to herself.

"This man, his demeanor disagrees with my feelings for him," Rory said.

"It's not our place to like him or not, Uncle Rory," Jack added.

"True, Jack, she is the one who will have to live with him, no?" Rory's constant smile grew bigger into a pearly white, toothy grin. The familiar squeak of the front screen door announced the visitor.

"Come on in, lover boy!" They heard Erin say.

"Why thank you, my dear," an unfamiliar voice replied.

Is that a southern accent? Erin found herself a Johnny Reb?

"Pardon me if I throw up in my mouth a little,"

Rory covered his mouth.

"It's not that bad, Rory," Jack corrected the foreman.

"Is it sappy?" Rose asked Rory. He nodded.

"Like a maple tree in spring," Rory replied. Rose feigned shooting herself in the head with a finger and a cock of her thumb. She rolled her eyes and bent her neck in response. The couple walked into the dining room, hand in hand.

"Hello, Chad," Peggy said. Uncle Rory didn't fib. Chad Gowing stood a hair shy of six feet tall, making him shorter than Erin if she wore heels. He shaved his head, which highlighted his crystal blue eyes. Chad's arms bore tribal tattoos from the wrists past the sleeves of his polo shirt.

"Mrs. McEntire, Mr. McEntire, Uncle Rory," he nodded to each person in turn. Erin sat down, patting the seat of her beau's placement, next to their mother and across from Rose.

"This is my sister, Rose. Rosie, this is Chad." Erin held her fiancé as she introduced her sibling to him. He extended a hand to shake, which Rose accepted.

"Pleased to meet you," Rose said. She didn't like him. The look of him, his smell, touching his cold and clammy hand, all of it skeeved her out. Yet, for as much as his presence revolted Rose, she remained polite.

"Likewise," Chad responded. The accent of a

southern gentleman indeed rolled off his lips. It sounded like Georgia, or maybe Alabama, to Rose, confirming her suspicions.

Likewise? Who the fuck uses that word anymore?

"I like your pentagram."

"It's a pentacle, and thanks," Rose's instincts told her not to trust this guy one bit.

"He's writing a book about the French-Indian War," Erin added. She kissed him on the cheek.

"Well, the Seven Years War. The first world war, some say. It encompassed all the known continents and hemispheres. The North American theater is quite interesting. Some of the bloodiest battles took place in New York."

"So why here? The Mohawk Valley and Lake George area were where the action was then," Rose knew her family history.

"I've been studying the area's genealogy, anthropologically. That means I'm tracing back old families in the area and their impact on the war."

"Families like our family," Erin interjected, "I met him in a MyFace group, and he wanted to interview me at first. He saw Daddy's collection of old guns on the fireplace behind me on a video screen. So, I told him to come down here. And then we fell in love, didn't we, Chaddy baby."

"We sure did. I thought you'd never invite me down. We talked for at least a year," Chad kissed

Erin deeply.

How could she be seriously marrying this guy? The saccharine sweetness of her sister with this man turned Rose's stomach. Chad broke the kiss and continued overdoing the casual knowledge dump.

"This area has a rich history, the Cardiff Giant, for example, which created a media frenzy across the nation. And did you know this isn't the first time this region has had an unsolved murder spree? Back in nineteen-"

"Yes, we know the history around these parts, Chad," Peggy cut him off, "our family, we've been here a long time. Ever since the famine in Ireland," the girls' mother noted, placing the attention on herself and away from her daughter's embarrassing display of affection, "A very long time, now, indeed." Peggy put her hand to her face and sighed. Jack shook his head in disapproval.

"A lot of Irish Americans came over then," Chad agreed.

"The Mac Tires were first, we weren't wanted back over there, so we left. We're Americans now, and we've fought in every war for freedom from oppression since," Jack added, saying more than either sister heard him say in years. "Can we finish dinner without you two pawing all over each other? I'd tell you more, that is unless you two want to go to a room and rut?" The sarcasm burned off Jack

McEntire's lips.

Rose kept her amusement at her father's dig to herself. Her father opening up as he did, a remarkable thing in and of itself, shocked her.

After dinner, Peggy served coffee. Erin snuggled up to her beau, and Rose sat next to her father. The family patriarch gathered his thoughts, but before Jack could add to the previous conversation, the police scanner sitting on a credenza came to life.

"Hey, Sarge? It's Jim Roth on Route 11 about half a mile from the Byrne Dairy going southbound back into Tinker's Falls."

"I'm here. Whatcha got Jimmy?" The dispatcher replied.

"Andy, you're not going to believe this. I think I ..." a long pause followed, then, *"Oh my god, I think I found another one. And it's a fucking mess."*

"Are you sure it's a person and not a deer?"

The nape hairs rose on Rose's neck as the State Trooper described the scene to his supervisor.

"Oh yeah, it's a person. It's so bad, Andy."

"How bad?"

"Really bad. Oh no, Andy, It's my cousin's neighbor. Tiffani Mason."

"How do you know?"

"She's staring at me, hanging between two trees with her lungs pulled out of her back and spread out like wings! And her eyes! She's missing her eyes, just like the last two girls! Oh, sweet fucking Jesu-"

Retching sounds filled the audio feed. Jack shook his head in disgust and switched off the scanner, having heard enough.

"I think I will go now," Rory said, breaking the silence, "the first light comes early." He stood and walked out of the dining room. Peggy followed him. His yellow rain slicker hung on a coat rack in the foyer.

"We'll see you in the morning, Uncle Rory," she kissed him on the cheek before he exited. He didn't have far to go. Rory's position allotted him a private loft suite in the barn. Peggy watched as their foreman walked away.

She surveyed their property, first looking to the left, then to the right, twice, as if she were preparing to cross the street. Satisfied nothing out of the ordinary might be lurking on the grounds, she closed the big oak door and turned the deadbolt. Its click resonated through the house, amplified by the occupants' silence.

6

Everyone went to their rooms, not wanting to discuss the latest victim in the murders. Bed usually came late for Jack and Peggy McEntire, and an empty nest full of their spawn made it later on this night. Once all their guests made it to their rooms, they allowed themselves to do the same.

"Who did you think you were fooling? You're a stupid son of a bitch," Jack McEntire said while he washed his hands in the half-bath's pedestal sink. He stared at his reflection in the vanity mirror. Jack's beard matched his short hair. Once a brilliant red, it faded over the decades into a smoky nest of curls. He snarled at himself, furrowed his brow, and turned away.

"Only crazy people or those with money in the bank talk to themselves," he heard his wife say.

"It's no secret I'm nuttier than squirrel crap," he laughed as he spoke. His wife always managed to keep his spirits high. Instead of drying his hands with a towel, Jack shook the water off them. It worked, mostly. He tied the sash of his tartan bathrobe and dried his hands off the rest of the way.

"I'm glad both of the girls are home," Peggy said. She sat on the edge of their bed in a frumpy, purple nightshirt, brushing her long hair. Streaks of white offset her black locks, giving the family matron a distinguished and wise appearance. Jack stepped out of the master bedroom's half bath and approached his wife.

"Hopefully, this Foothills Slasher nonsense will be put to rest," Jack added, "It's ugly what's come of it," Peggy frowned as Jack shook his head, "Ugly." He pursed his lips and returned to his Stoic demeanor.

"Is that a tear in your eye, John Joseph Junior?" She reached up to her husband's face and wiped away the droplet, "you haven't cried since-" Jack didn't let his wife finish her sentence. He placed a hand on each of Peggy's cheeks, pulled her face to his, and placed his lips on hers. It seemed to last forever.

"I love you, Margaret," Jack said, calling his wife by her birth name, after breaking the kiss. Peggy dropped her hairbrush, wrapped her arms around her husband, and held him tight.

"I love you, too, Jackie Mack," he smiled at hearing his childhood nickname, something not used in some time. Jack tipped his body, shifting the balance, forcing Peggy to fall onto the bed next to him. The couple held each other on the mattress until they fell asleep with their pajamas on.

7

Rose went straight to bed but couldn't sleep. The news of the latest murder didn't bother her. Truth be told, she expected it. Erin's boyfriend took all the enthusiasm for coming home out of her. Something troubled her about him, he didn't seem all there, almost aloof. Who gets engaged to someone after meeting them online? And only after a few days of actually seeing one another?

These thoughts invaded Rose's mind, and now she couldn't sleep. Tomorrow brought the last harvest. Traditionally, the family's feast followed, making for a long day and another reason to get some rest. But Rose tossed and turned for what seemed like hours before finally deciding to go downstairs and get some fresh air.

And chocolate milk.

Sweatpants became the order of the night. Rose complimented them with a t-shirt and hoodie. Slid her feet in slippers and pulled her hair back in a ponytail. Her phone sat in the charging cradle, and she left it there. She didn't use social media, nor did she plan on leaving the property.

Moments later Rose made her way to the kitchen to pour the glass of chocolate milk. She loved the beverage and knew she shouldn't drink it. It gave her the shits, every time. She savored every drop, making them worth the cramps and unladylike moments to come.

The porch welcomed her. The rain stopped, but she could still hear thunder in the distance. She wrapped up in the blanket from the parlor, to keep the chill off, and sat in one of the rockers, milk in hand. She sipped on the frigid milk, sighed after sucking down the last drop, and burped.

Memories flooded Rose, from before she moved. Dad used to take them up to the glider platform on Morgan Hill. He'd set up his telescope, and they'd marvel at the beauty of the moon and the neighboring planets.

The moon filled the sky, Venus stretching out beside it. Across the horizon, the crimson of Mars flickered. They fascinated Rose, the celestial bodies. She wished upon shooting stars, ever since her youth. Isolated deep in the countryside, without the ambient lights of cities to interfere, the stars lit the night.

The best view from their property stood near the

epicenter of the orchard. During summer, the bioluminescent flickering of fireflies created a terrestrial galaxy in the surrounding trees and fields. The scene mirrored what Rose saw in the sky above, a reminder of the spiral connecting all of it.

Fuck it. Rose decided. *It's not a far walk, and I could use the exercise!* Foothills Slasher or not. The odds of the killer being on their property were slim, at best. Rose set the glass down and stood. The orchards beckoned, tempting her with their solitude. She missed walking through them. She didn't come home to deny these simple pleasantries.

The rain-soaked the path earlier, making the trip a bit sloppier than Rose liked. Still, she soldiered on. She refused to allow a little water to prevent her from enjoying the smell of ripe apples and dying leaves. The stars lit the way.

8

When the rain stopped, the ambient noise of it falling on the metal barn roof faded away, and Rory woke from dreams of his long-forgotten youth. Too much of Mrs. McEntire's apple juice during dinner traveled through his body, now it knocked on his bladder's door. The cold, linoleum flooring of his apartment curled his toes and sent a shiver up his spine, increasing his desire to piss.

Each step caused the urge to grow, forcing the old man to grab his pecker through his red and black checkered pajama pants, and pinch it off. At his age, the bladder wasn't what it used to be. The proximity of the half-bath and shower to his bedroom in his apartment prevented an accident. He sighed in relief as a never-ending stream of urine exited his body.

When it finally ended, Rory shook his unit dry and washed his hands and face. He could feel the draw of sleep, calling him back to the memories of yore. He closed his eyes, knowing the layout of his living space, and walked blind back to his bed.

Brannigan thought the light knocking on his door might be from the dream his brain played out. When it increased in volume, he realized the knocking indeed existed in the real world. Rory again opened his eyes and shook the cobwebs out.

"One minute," Rory mumbled. No one answered, but the knocking stopped. The foreman changed his direction and shuffled his feet to the apartment door. With half-closed eyes, he turned the knob, "Hell-"

The door flew open. The knob cracked into the foreman's extended hand, breaking three fingers. His wrist bent back with the door's momentum, slamming into his shoulder and forehead. The blow stunned him and sent Brannigan tumbling to the floor. He cracked his head off the linoleum. Instead of knocking him out, it created a moment of clarity. He opened his eyes in time to see the flash of polished steel coming out of the darkness.

He knew this sword. Jack McEntire's claymore, brought over from the old world.

Wolf Cleaver.

He threw an arm up as a shield. The blade struck Rory's exposed limb and bit into the skin. He could hear the snapping bones in his appendage. The ancient sword half-cut, half-broke, his ulna bone from the force. The blow sent the blade slicing through his radius without any resistance. Blood jetted out of the stump, covering the floor.

A gloved hand grabbed the wounded limb and pulled it to a face, obscured by the darkness. Slurping and sucking sounds followed as the blade swung in a high arc and struck Rory in the groin. It carried up through him, the razor-sharp edge ignoring bone and muscle along the way.

The human body is incapable of withstanding this much duress. Before the steel bisected his lungs and severed the arteries and veins, Rory Brannigan's brain registered a critical hit. A microsecond later, the organs in his body took their genetic suicide pills. Then they exited the premises, spilling onto the floor.

9

Near the center of the first ringlet of apple trees, something moved behind Rose, catching her attention. She turned around and saw a shadow flutter in the grove, startling her. The unexpected presence caused her heart to pound in her chest.

"Mom? Dad?" She asked. The shadow stopped. "Erin?" The shadow launched across the path into a pocket of darkness. "Who's there?" Lightning lit up the night sky, flashing through the trees and filling the land with brilliance for a fraction of a second.

Long enough for Rose to see someone-something-*hiding behind a tree.*

Her heart raced, beating in her chest. She ran. The shadow moved in tandem, falling across her path, creating a translucent barrier. It stopped at the edge of the path and Rose knew whatever stalked her, now stood in behind a tree.

Bogeyman my ass! I'm not ready for this! She thought. The barn stood nearby, closer than the family home. She could lock the doors in there and call into the house and warn her sleeping family. Halfway there she remembered her phone and mentally kicked herself for leaving it in the bedroom.

Fuck!

She didn't turn around. The barn! She ran as fast as her slippered feet would allow. The grass, wet from the rain earlier, made running difficult. She slipped and almost fell following the curve of the orchard's trail. As she tried to regain her footing, the dark of night moved, and Rose realized the shadow found her.

"Boo, Bee-otch!" Erin screamed as she jumped out from behind a blooming Mountain Ash tree, blocking her sister's path. Rose slid into her, knocking both to the ground. The pair tumbled into the leaves, grass, and apples.

"You asshole!" Rose chastised her sister, "you scared me to death!"

"Hardly! It'll take more than that to take you down, you are my sister, after all." Erin started laughing. Rose nodded and joined in the mirth. Rose loved these banters with her sister. They reminded her of when things were simpler. She missed those days.

The sisters laid side by side in the cold wet grass, staring up at the sky. They watched the remaining clouds fly through the air, catching streaks of the Draconids in their peripheral vision, as the space rocks struck the earth's atmosphere. Rose made wishes for each one.

"I'm so happy to be home," Rose said, watching the fog of her breath disappear with her words.

"There's no place like home," Erin agreed.

Rose closed her eyes, satisfied all was well. The familiar cramping flooded her lower abdomen. Rose clenched her ass cheeks and squinted, her whole body going rigid. She knew what might be coming, and she prayed it would go away.

It didn't.

The gurgling in Rose's bowels shifted and moved. Only partially sure it wouldn't include any solid or liquid material, she let it out. A wet, clapping foghorn erupted from her ass.

"What the hell?" Erin said and elbowed her sister, "you got into the chocolate milk, didn't you! Damn, girl. It smells like you licked a can of Alpo clean. Say excuse me."

"Give me a chance to-"

A terrible crashing sound filled the night. A moment later, a banshee's wail pierced their ears, and the sisters knew the serenity lied. They hopped to their feet. The noise, the screaming, came from their home.

ST ROOSTER BOOKS

10

A rattling from down the hall stirred Jack and Peggy McEntire from their slumber. Somebody in the house faced getting their ass kicked by inanimate objects of some sort. Judging from the incredible racket being made, the objects were winning the battle.

"Can you go see if someone needs some help?" Peggy asked her husband, "It's probably Erin's boyfriend. We can't have him snooping around here. I don't trust him; he was eying too many of my antiques."

"That's what you call them now?" Jack quipped, "you cling to the past too much, gotta get with the times, woman."

"Says the man with a martial museum hanging on the wall of our family room." Jack laughed in response.

"My antiques still work."

"Yes, they do," Peggy squeezed her husband's groin, "now go help them. When you come back, I might have some appraising of my own to do." Jack kissed his wife on the cheek, gave her a playful growl, and left their bedroom.

No lights were on, anywhere in the house. Jack found this odd. The clamor grew in volume, coming from the kitchen area. Instead of making his presence known, Jack opted for the stealth approach. A thief? Or worse? The hair rose on his nape, warning him of danger.

Could someone (something?) *be in the house?* He wondered. The noise abated; Jack could hear movement. Labored breathing, almost a panting, grew in intensity. He remained quiet. Startling a robber could be dangerous to everyone in the house, making it the last thing he wanted to do.

Breath ... step. Jack reminded himself. *Breath ... step.*

Hugging the wall, he crept down the hallway. He tip-toed, wary of squeaky floorboards under the carpet, stepping on the balls of his bare feet.

Breath ... The shadows moved. Jack froze. A glowing streak of red swooshed across the darkness.

"Jack! Look out!" Peggy, watching from the sanctity of their bedroom, screamed. He turned his head back to her, seeing her run down the hall towards him.

"Peg?" Jack watched his wife run to him, her desperate, terrified face betraying an unseen horror. He whipped his head around to see his claymore, held by a mystery adversary, driving toward him.

Instead of dodging, Jack charged. Peggy grabbed him from behind, pulling him backward. The effort came too late.

The sword's tip pierced her arm at the wrist. The steel drove through the flesh and bone, severing her hand, before stabbing into Jack's exposed chest.

Peggy jerked her arm back and screeched in pain, falling to the carpet. Her arm behaved like a garden hose with a kink. Blood spurted out of the stump in time with her beating heart, spraying the walls, ceiling, and floor.

"You'll pay for this, you fuck!" Jack challenged his assailant as the sword blade impaled him. The force drove him back, into the wall, but Jack gave zero fucks. He reached up with both hands and clamped them on the sword. It did nothing to stop the blade from sliding through his chest and out his back, into the wall.

Pinned, Jack flailed his limbs, kicking and swinging, trying to hit his assailant. The length of the great sword kept him out of reach.

The attacker twisted the blade. Bone crunched as a four-inch hole bored through his sternum. Blood squirted down the blade. The murderer twisted the sword until it snagged on something in the wall.

Jack McEntire made one last, futile attempt to strike his murderer.

He failed.

"Jack!" Peggy screamed. The woman lunged down the hall, past the attacker. She didn't dare look at the murderer. She knew the answer. Instead, she ran into the kitchen. She uncovered her stump and blood squirted out, covering the bay window with a crimson coat.

Peggy turned on the gas stove's front burner. Three clicks and the blue flame came to life, illuminating the area in an azure haze. She opened the freezer door and pulled out the icemaker's tray and slammed it on the counter next to the stovetop.

Peggy McEntire stuffed the stump on her arm into the fire and screamed bloody murder.

She yanked it back out, only to push it into the ice tray. She screamed again and wrapped a dish towel and oven mitt around the blistered and cauterized stump where her hand used to be.

Fuck you, asshole. Peggy thought. *You picked the wrong house.*

The killer heard the scream and followed, stomping down the hall, but instead of going to the kitchen, they stopped at the family room.

Peggy stood by the stove, shaking from shock, blood loss, and fear. A pair of metal clicks verified her worst-case scenario.

The guns. They're loaded. Jack keeps them ready.

"Fuck you!" She yelled in defiance and dropped to the floor behind the kitchen island. A second set of clicks answered her.

A chorus of thunderous roars filled the house with smoke and fire. The round struck the bay window, shattering it. Peggy saw her opportunity, got up, and ran for the foyer and the exit. Halfway there, something grabbed her by the back of the neck and threw her across the room, into the door.

The force of the blow blew the door out. Splinters and pieces scattered across the steps and knocked over the jack o' lanterns. Peggy McEntire landed on the floor, dazed.

11

Running as fast as she could in the wet grass while wearing slippers, Rose fell behind Erin by a few strides. She caught up with her sister at the edge of the driveway.

Disaster greeted the siblings from the porch of the McEntire homestead. A quarter of the front door hung by a hinge; the remaining pieces sat scattered across the deck. A gaping hole rested in the front of the house where the bay window once provided a view of the orchard.

The moon reflected a glistening black ichor coating the walls of the house interior. It dripped from the window frame, pooling on the ground. One of the jack o' lanterns lay on its side next to a puddle, the candle still burning.

"Mom! Dad! Chad!" Erin screamed. Rose grabbed her arm.

"What are you doing? Do you want to let everyone know we're here?"

"Why not? Mom!" She called out again.

"But what if-"

"What if what?"

"What if it's the Foothills Slasher? Look at the porch! Is that blood?"

"Are you serious? You are, aren't you?" Erin, despite the circumstances, stifled a giggle.

"This isn't funny, Erin. Excuse me for being paranoid. But can't you see this?" Rose pointed at the house. They turned their heads in unison revealing their mother. Peggy McEntire stood in the open doorway. Blood covered her face. "Mom?" Rose said, shocked to see her there in such a condition.

"Girls?" Peggy said, making eye contact with her daughters.

"What happened to you?" Erin screamed. The girls picked back up their race to the house in earnest.

"No!" Peggy threw her hands up. Rose saw the wrapped arm and wondered why it was shorter than the other. "Run away! Run for your-" Peggy's words stopped short. The McEntire matron arched her back and tumbled onto the porch and down the steps.

A meat cleaver from the kitchen stuck into her back.

Rose and Erin screamed a chorus of terror.

Chad Gowing, wearing only his boxers, stood behind Peggy's prone body. A crimson sheen covered him. He saw the sisters, too, and made eye contact with Rose. A shiver of fear ran up her spine.

Did he just kill our mother? Where's Dad?

"Hello, ladies," Chad said to the sisters, behaving as if all were normal, "pardon me, one second," he reached down and pulled the cleaver out of Peggy's back and sighed, "There we go. If you're looking for Dad, he's hanging out in the den."

"Not tonight, Satan! Not tonight!" Rose said and took Erin's hand. She kicked off her slippers, and the pair bolted, "fuck this!"

"Oh, come on! Now I've got to chase you!"

The sisters ran away from Erin's blood-soaked fiancé, back to the safety of the darkness covering the trees. They knew the orchard, they knew where to hide, and the barn beyond. He didn't. This gave the siblings an advantage.

They hoped.

12

Twisted shadows formed in the moonlight embracing the barren apple trees of the orchard. Rose and Erin sprinted through the trees, hoping to reach the barn. Once inside, they could lock the doors, secure them, and call for help.

They didn't have to look behind to know Chad pursued them.

He did.

The grass, wet from the rain earlier, made running difficult. Both women slipped and almost fell twice before reaching the Elysium of the barn. Once inside, Rose slammed the doors behind her and twisted the lock. Twin deadbolts dropped into their slots and secured the doors.

"You brought the fucking bogeyman to our house? What were you fucking thinking?" Rose berated her sister.

"It looks like I did," Erin confessed, "but that's

not the problem right now. Staying alive is. Now help me find a weapon to fucking kill his ass with!" Rose joined her sister in the survival scavenger hunt. The workmen's jackets, hanging on pegs along a wall and a time clock, reminded her, they were not alone.

"Hey, doesn't Uncle Rory stay here?"

"Holy shit, you're right! I forgot!"

"Then let's find him!" Rose and Erin ran to the back of the building, looking for the foreman. A loud bang on the front door startled them, reminding them a virtual timer counted down until Chad reached the barn.

"His apartment is in the loft, up here." Erin led Rose up the stairs leading to the barn's expansive second floor. The sisters reached the top and stopped. Before them, a bisected display of utter carnage decorated the loft in splinters of wood and gore.

Two halves of Rory Brannigan hung from a rafter, each dangling from an ankle. A length of intestine, drawn from his eviscerated bowels, wrapped around the beam and each of the foreman's feet.

Surprisingly, little blood stained the floor below his carcass. Instead, his decapitated head rested next to a forearm and hand on a stool under the body. A death grin greeting the sisters. Both stood frozen in place, terror coursing through their bodies.

Erin screamed.

Rose couldn't.

Something slammed into the doors for a third time, breaking them from their trance, and they ran back down the stairs. Another blow came as they reached the first floor, shaking the door frame, startling the girls more. They watched as a tomahawk blade bit through the steel door, once, then a second time.

"Come out, come out, little piggies," Chad growled from the other side of the door, his accent dripping off the words he spoke. Mad laughter followed.

"Piggies? Oh, if you only knew, motherfucker! Fuck you, you sucked in bed. Mushroom dick!" Erin screamed in defiance, jumping back from the locked doors.

"No, fuck you. The lock, it won't work, sugar. You invited me to the property, or did you forget? You're kind of stuck with me."

"Invited you? What the fuck are you talking about? What do you want with us? Better yet, what did you do to our mother and father?" Rose shouted back. Erin shrugged her shoulders and shook her head. She busied about the barn, looking for anything she could use as a weapon.

"I think you saw what I did to the bitch, but before that, I stuck your old man to the wall with his claymore. He makes the room, matches the rug like a champ. Now, I want your blood, sugar. Like that girl at the carnival, so sweet and almost pure. I ate her tongue while I sucked the blood out. She had some impurities. Someone in her family fucked a plebe, kept the beast, and raised it like a human, spoiled that royal blood," he slapped the doors. They shook in the frame, "and you loved it when I ate you out during your heat, your blood, so pure. The purest I've tasted in decades. Then I figured it out. Enough fucking around, the big bad wolf is hungry, and he's coming in!"

Gowing punched the barn door with both fists, each strike sent a bolt of thunder echoing across the property. He punctured the wood, and Rose and Erin watched helplessly as Chad grabbed the locking bar and ripped the doors open. Metal squealed in agony, unable to resist Chad's strength.

The man stood before the sisters, his muscles rippling, triumphant in his feat of strength. Tribal tattoos on his arms covered his upper torso. His eyes glowed red and hateful. Erin held a pitchfork in both hands, warding Chad off with its tines.

"I'm not fucking around, I'll stab you, Chad!" Erin threatened him with the tool. Frantic, Rose ruffled through a toolbox looking for any sort of weapon. She chose a clawed hammer.

"Please, do your worst, little pig. I followed your lineage here from the Old World, through war after war across the globe, seeking the purest royal blood." He lunged at Erin. She thrust the pitchfork at him. He dodged to the side.

Rose jumped on his back. She swung the hammer down, hard as she could, onto Chad's head. It grazed the crown of his skull and deflected off the side. Rose felt a stinger in her hand, and the hammer flew across the room. He grabbed the woman's arm with a free hand and tossed her off him.

Chad snatched the impromptu weapon from Erin on the return swing. The woman held tight and jerked toward him, allowing Gowing to strike his former lover in the face with the back of his hand. He twisted the handle, snapped it in half, and tore the pitchfork out of Erin's grasp.

A jagged splinter tore her T-shirt open, and she fell to the floor, on her back. Her head snapped onto the concrete and dazed her. Erin closed her eyes and shook her head. Around her neck, two eyes hung on a leather cord, staring back at Rose and Chad.

What the fuck is that? Rose thought. Chad didn't see it, or if he did, he didn't care. Instead, he continued to run his mouth.

"All this fuckery is making me famished, ladies," the killer paused and licked his lips, "who will it be fir-"

A wolf howled and drowned out Chad's taunting.

A fog lifted in Rose's mind.

"You keep throwing that word *wolf* around like you know what it means," Erin said. Rose pointed over Chad's shoulder to the house.

In the distance, a football field away, Jack and Peggy McEntire stood on the porch of their house. This wouldn't be out of the ordinary, except Chad claimed to have murdered their father. They watched him kill their mother.

Or did they.

It is worth noting the family patriarch and his wife stood side by side, buck naked. Blue stripes of paint spiraled around their bodies, mixed with their own blood. It gave them a terrifying appearance.

Perplexed, Chad returned his attention to the sisters who didn't behave like prey.

Because they weren't.

They never were.

"Did you say your prayers tonight, Digger Do?" Erin asked her former fiancé. She kicked off her sneakers as she ripped off what remained of her t-shirt, revealing blue ink painted across her body in the same spiral patterns as her parents. Her gray eyes glowed with a soft amber hue.

Rose followed suit, cast aside her clothing, and joined her sky-clad sister. Matching cobalt stripes and knots decorated Rose's skin.

Their eyes glowed amber and together they answered their father's howl.

Chad stepped back a few feet and ran off, into the apple orchard. Rose and Erin gave the vampire a moment to build false confidence before taking off after him.

The Last Harvest was underway.

13

A foggy haze hung over the orchard, the remnants of the previous day's storms. Chad Gowing ran for his unlife through this circular labyrinth of trees. He tried cutting through the brush and discovered the McEntires grew more than apple trees.

Mountain Ash, brought from Ireland and blooming with bright berries, stood between rows of Macintosh trees. Peggy loved the flowers so much; she named her baby after them. Rose bushes, with deep red flowers and long, wicked thorns, were hidden between the trees. The McEntires knew the power of *witchwood* and its effects on the tick-like, vampiric beings they called a Digger Do. It made a near-impenetrable barrier for the blood-sucker and gave him no recourse but to follow the maze.

Erin and Rose McEntire chased the parasite.

The girls knew the orchard well, having hunted on it for decades. Erin split off from her sibling, weaving through the trees as she bounded away. Rose went the other direction, creating a pincer. Their goal? To herd the prey to the center of the grove. They didn't want to kill him.

Not yet.

The cobalt ink covering the McEntires worked to camouflage the girls in the trees. They watched him from the shadows, ensuring he continued their desired pathway. Tracking him proved to be an easy task. He made more than enough noise running away, plodding through the wet grass.

Rose laughed at Chad's cowardice. When he believed the McEntires to be mundane and naïve, he expressed a bit of appreciable bravado. But now, with the effects of their obfuscation spell wearing off, Chad knew he was fucked. He faced a family who lived up to their surname, allowing him to show the true nature of all parasites.

A bottom-feeding, shit-licking, Digger Do.

Chad reached an opening in the trees and bushes. At the epicenter stood a trio of standing stones, carved in Celtic runes. Sconces with torches lit the area. The flickering flames created dancing fireflies, hovering around the giant, vertical rocks. An altar slab greeted him at the forefront of the slabs.

He bolted across the field, past the stones and

altar. Before Chad could move another step, the McEntire sisters were on him, pouncing out of the tree line and surrounding him.

Gowing hissed, barring fangless teeth. Rose jumped at him, grabbing him by an arm. He struggled with her long enough for Erin to leap and capture his legs. Chad fought back with the strength of twenty men, thrashing about, but to no avail. The girls held him down with grips of steel.

14

Jack and Peggy arrived, dried blood contrasting the blue ink. Rose noticed the flesh around the stab wound in Jack's chest, still stitching itself back together. Her mother's stump now scabbed over, the veins and arteries sealed. She grabbed hold of Chad with her good hand.

Together, the family carried their reluctant prey. Chad kicked and squirmed as they carried him across the field to the heart of the labyrinth of spiral rings making up the McEntire apple orchard.

The McEntires threw their sacrifice on the slab. Erin and Rose held his arms down, and Peggy held his legs with her one good hand, as Jack secured Chad using chains braided with silver. They burned into his undead skin, sizzling. He screeched in agony. Erin pulled Chad's boxers off and stuffed them in his mouth. It shut him up.

"We don't want your Digger Do blood. It's

polluted. We only want your meat, it sustains us, allows us to live on and on," Rose whispered in Chad's ear, "we've been trapping your kind here for centuries."

"You're a tough one, son," Jack said, "I thought you might've had me back in the house," he rubbed his chest, "this is the first time in a hundred years we've had to sacrifice our kin to hide our intent, but the *Eyes of Abhartach* allowed us to hide the harvest from you," Jack fingered the knotted cord tied around his neck and the pair of eyeballs it held.

Similar necklaces adorned Peggy and Erin. The knotting on each differed. Now Rose understood the sacrifices they made to catch this bastard. Their local kin who they'd never forget, the women sacrificed to trap this son of a bitch for the harvest.

Never is a long time when you can live forever, Rose's thoughts knew the curse of empathy. The melancholy, a tithe paid as penance for her family's continued existence. Sleepless nights measured with the weight of innocent lives. The knowledge irked her.

"I still can't believe you brought the bogeyman, and a Digger Do at that, into our house," Rose said to Erin, turning her frustration on her sibling.

"Digger Do's are women. And besides, Mom said I could," Erin looked to her mother for support.

"Don't look at me," Peggy told her older daughter, "You said yes when he proposed."

"Does this mean I have to call the DJ and cancel the reception hall?" Erin asked in her typical deadpan delivery. Rose couldn't be sure if her sister was serious or not.

"I suppose it's for the best," Peggy replied to her daughter, playing along, "There's no way I'm having any parties until the hand grows back. I hate looking like a raccoon who got caught in a trap."

"You still look sexy to me, Stubby," Jack teased his wife. She thrust the arm in the air.

"You know what I'm doing with my ghost finger right now?"

"Ayup," Jack replied, "Thanks for telling me I'm number one, baby. Alright, Rosie, the pig is ready, you're *Cathain* this year. It's your turn to cut the meat." The Curadmir, the champion's portion, awarded to the bravest warrior in the clan, the *Cathain*. This year, Rose earned the honor by default.

"Thanks, Dad," Rose replied, smiled, and moved to the foot of the altar next to her mother.

"Don't forget to leave a bite for Conner," Peggy said to her daughter.

"Don't worry, I will," a shooting star broke through the clouds, lighting the night. Rose cocked her head to the sky with her family and watched. It's almost as if the heavens answered her mother's words.

"The god provides," Jack said, crossing himself.

His family answered in kind.

Rose lurched forward and arched her back, a grimace of agony crossing her face.

The power of the Mórrígan coursed through her.

Her shoulders arched; her legs stiffened. She felt the hair growing from her skin. A jolt of pain shot through her spine, and Rose twisted her back, falling to the ground. She fell into a trance, allowing the metamorphosis to flow, as she did every year at this time.

A long, clawed hand slapped onto the slab next to Chad's foot. Then another followed suit. Chad struggled, his eyeballs bulging in his head, the fear of his mortality settling in. Before Chad's prone body arose a vision from Hell.

Rose's transformation shifted her into a gigantic, hairy, wolfish hominoid. The beast-woman's black coat shimmered in the torchlight. Bipedal and hunched over, she flexed muscular arms and legs. A long, fanged snout now protruded from her face. Her eyes, yellow and black, showed no human empathy.

The human and wolf hybrid pounced on the prone vampyr. With two swift cuts, sharp claws opened the veins in his forearms Chad squirmed in agony as the flesh sliced open. Blood poured from the wounds, gushing into the reservoir channel encircling the slab.

The wolfwoman watched as the red halo around

Chad's eyes faded with the blood exiting his body. When he finally stopped fighting and the light went out, she knew gravity did its job and drained the parasite dry.

It didn't take long.

Rose opened her mouth wide and bit down into Chad Gowing's exsanguinated shoulder. Her tongue tasted the delicious meat. She shook her head and ripped a chunk free.

A flash of lightning filled the sky, and a wind picked up speed. The torches flickered, and their fireflies dispersed. The distant thunder answered, rolling across the hills. High above their heads, across from the moon, Mars twinkled in the sky. Jack McEntire howled to the Goddess of War, and his bitches sang along.

Nope, Rose McEntire thought, savoring the morsel, *there's no way in hell I'll ever miss a trip home for this. Not ever.*

2: IMBOLC

DOGS DON'T LIE

ST ROOSTER BOOKS

ST ROOSTER BOOKS

DOGS DON'T LIE

1

Each year, as the last of the dead leaves are blown from the skeletons of trees, winter sneaks into the Tully Foothills. Freezing rains ride the wind across Lake Ontario, heralding the flurries to come with the Longest Night. If you listen carefully, you might hear a banshee's cry echo through the hillsides, as the cold settles in.

Overnight, the region transforms into a

prehistoric anachronism of ice and snow, forcing the residents to find shelter within their homes. Protected from the elements, these souls bundle up by the hearth for warmth and wait for spring.

Not everyone hides away from the winter's bite. The region breeds a hearty lot, tempered by the seasonal changes. Life goes on, despite the weather. Deer, rabbits, foxes, and raccoons compete for scraps. Most birds have flown south, but the crows. Like the other animals, they stay, to forage the meager bits available.

Hard-working people commute to their jobs while the adventurous traverse snowmobile trails, snowshoe pathways, and ski slopes. For some, the adventure is part of their job, especially those working outside the restrictions of the laws of society.

Deep within the foothills, under the shadow of Morgan Hill, a trio of hikers makes their way through the rows of evergreens surrounding Sullivan Hollow State Park and Morgan Hill. The trio is mostly dressed for the occasion, with thick winter coats, hats, and gloves. Empty backpacks adorn their backs. They wear boots, but denim jeans are their choice of legwear. Anyone with any cold-weather hiking skills will tell you this is a poor choice. Denim is cotton, and cotton can kill.

The Stackhouses, Steve and Rhonda, possess no outdoor skills. Dickie Pecker, their associate, has never been in the woods before. As a result, they are unaware of the danger they are in. Inner-city folk, Steve's Wranglers hang down his ass to the middle of his boxers. A Confederate Navy Jack bandana is tied to his head like a skull cap. Rhonda wears more makeup than the job requires. It annoys Steve, who can see the line on her jaw where the facial paint ends.

Sometimes she reminds me of a drag queen, he told Crip once. If only Steve knew what Rhonda said about him in confidence with Crip. Much of it referenced Steve's shortcomings in the bedroom, or how cheap the son of bitch is. Take her wedding ring, for example. A thin silver band with what might be a fake ruby on top. She never checked, afraid of learning her assumptions may be true.

Out of the three of them, Crip shouldn't be out in the woods walking around. His ataxia made sure to remind him of this.

Born with Cerebral Palsy, Richard 'Dickie' Pecker earned the moniker of Crip in high school, and it stuck. As a result of his chaotic gait, and errant right arm, he much preferred the socially inappropriate name to the one on his birth certificate. Ever the opportunist, he frequently used his body's ticks as a pick-up line with women.

"Hey baby, ever wonder what a man with a naturally vibrating cock was like?" opened more hotel room doors for Mr. Pecker than you might

think. His double entendre first and last names likely assisted his amorous endeavors. Possessing a giant cock didn't hurt his cause, either.

The backwoods of the Tully Foothills, however, are not a hotel's carpeted flooring, nor do they come equipped with elevators. Crip could navigate a king-size bed with ease, but he could barely walk down the aisle of Wal*Mart, let alone the uneven, snowpack of the forest.

The adventure started out innocent enough. Steve called all the customers walking through his apartment looking for dime bags friends. One of these friends, with the bullshit nickname of Mac Cool, told him of a weed jackpot. A large, unprotected stash of marijuana. Pounds, cured and ready for the taking. The only catch? You had to hike through Sullivan Hollow State Park to find the barn it's stashed in.

Their quest ceased being fun when they lost the GPS signal, and their phones went dead. Steve, Rhonda, and Crip now faced incredible odds working against them. An hour of wandering in the forest on a midwinter's day is a challenge for any fit hiker. For this trio of miscreants, it's a losing battle of endurance.

"This is some Blair Witch shit I didn't want to be part of, for fuck's sake, Steve. I should be home watching Daytona, fuckin' bitches!" Crip says. Each step he takes is a labor in the snowpack.

"If we keep moving north, we'll hit Route 80 and the barn," Steve says, "we'll be there soon."

"That's what you said an hour ago, motherfucker, before we hiked up the side of a fucking mountain," Crip doesn't mince his words, "how do you know we're going north?"

"The sun, it's to our right, so this way is north," Steve points ahead.

"You better be right. This shit better be worth it."

"Pounds of weed, dried and ready for us to take. I trust my guy."

"You trust your guy," Crip snorts a giggle after he speaks, "and nobody is there, right?"

"Right. Nobody is there."

"Would you two stop your bitching?" Rhonda pipes in, "my feet and my nose are cold."

"Don't worry. We're almost there, baby," Steve says to his wife.

"Right. You keep saying that, Steve," Rhonda scolds her husband.

"Ya know, fuck you. Really. I'm trying to make us a buck here. Wouldn't you like to go on that cruise?"

"You know I do."

"Then shut the fuck up, both of you, and let's focus on finding the fucking trees, okay?" Steve says.

"There's trees all around, you can see them,

right?" Crip interjects. Steve gives Crip the finger, he returns the gesture, and they continue on.

They walk in silence for about five minutes. After crossing a small hill, it becomes evident something other than trees and snow lies ahead. At the crest, they see the forest clears.

A vast, snow-covered field is revealed. A junkyard, riddled with a few dozen cars, lies ahead on the path. Further beyond, a large, blue barn can be seen on the horizon.

"I told you motherfuckers it would be there!" Steve says and the trio of illicit treasure hunters run down the hill.

2

Adjacent to the barren cornfields, lies an orchard of apple and mountain ash. Rings of trees spread out from a central apex, mirroring ripples on a pond, following a spiraling irrigation moat. Vast acres of corn fields, now barren and covered in snow, border the eastern side of the orchard.

The waters of Spruce Pond, surrounded by the tall evergreens, rest across a private road that shares the same name. The road ends at a modest split-level ranch, which sits abreast of the orchard near a large blue barn. A pair of signs, one on Route 11 and the other between the barn and the home, mark the property as "Mac-Tire Farm & Orchard, Est. 1748."

Inside the slate blue ranch, Jack and Peggy McEntire sit at their dining room table. They drink hot cider from ceramic mugs, and watch the flames dance off burning logs in a fireplace, waiting for dusk to come.

The family patriarch is a burly man, with a thick red beard and dark, deep-set eyes. He keeps his curly head of hair in a brush cut. His wife is the light to his darkness. The McEntire clan matron's ebony tresses fall past her shoulders, into the middle of her back. Highlighted by more than a few stripes of white and gray, the latter strands match Peggy's eyes.

An old telephone rings, vibrating in its cradle on the wall. A rotary dial face stares back at Peggy, who answers the phone.

"Hello?" There is a brief pause as the person on the other end of the line speaks, "Oh, hi Rory," another pause, "okay. I'll tell Jack. We'll see you soon," she hangs the phone back in its cradle, "that was Rory, he's on his way with dinner."

"He's got it?" Jack asks his wife; a surprised look covers his face.

"Yes," she replies, raising her eyebrows as she nods, a smirk across her face, and sits back down at the table, "there's always one."

"Aye, funny how that works, love. The calendars of men may change, but the sun and the moon, they're constant," Jack says, then takes another sip of his cider before asking his wife, "Speaking of which, what did the groundhog do down in

Pennsyltucky today?"

"He saw his shadow," she replies, then stirs her cider with a spoon, "and it scared the little fucker shitless."

"That's good, I suppose. Ya sure it wasn't all the bullshit pomp and circumstance going on? Those cameras and lights? Kind of hard not to see your shadow."

"Naw," Peggy shakes her head, "they put the chicken shit bastard on a stump just as the sun broke. He squealed pretty loud. Conner would have gotten a kick out of it. He loved woodchucks."

"Of course, he did. You would too if your birthday was on Groundhog Day," Jack adds.

"Not everything is a joke, you know, dear husband," Peggy scowls at her husband, her words biting with each syllable.

"I didn't say it was," Jack responds to his wife's change in tone by doing the same, "you know how I feel about," he stops and pushes his mug aside in anger. A tear forms in his eye and his lip quivers, "it crushes me, too!"

Peggy sees the grief in her husband's face and chooses not to push the matter. She holds his hand on the table, soothing him. The duo remains silent, listening to the crackle of the fire until the logs turn black. Outside the bay window looking across the property, the sun can be seen hovering over the western horizon.

The sound of a single gunshot outside, in the distance, breaks the moment.

"I think it's time to go," Peggy says.

A second shot follows a minute later.

"I think you're right," Jack agrees and stands up...

3

A rusted-out blue Chevette crosses the path through the junkyard, blocking Steve, Rhonda, and Crip's path of least resistance. Stuck into the ground next to the car stands a POSTED sign declaring *'No Trespassing! Violators WILL be shot.'* The Chevy's remaining blue paint lost the battle against the elements years ago, but the windows remained pristine. Until today.

"Shot my fucking ass!" Steve throws a snowball at the sign and misses, instead he connects with the side windshield of the derelict compact car. The impact shattered the safety glass into a thousand bits. They hear the echo of the shatter return from across the field.

"Are you fucking stupid? Someone might hear that! Do you know what quiet is? The whole reason we hiked over a fucking mountain was so no one knew we were coming, and you go and ring a fucking doorbell!" Crip yells at Steve.

"Fuck you, I'll do as I please!" Steve gives Crip the finger, again, before bending down to form another snowball. He keeps padding in his hands, crushing it down into an ice ball.

"What the fuck is that?" Rhonda asks.

"What's what?" Steve replies to his wife.

"Hanging off the rearview mirror in the car," she points. Steve and Crip can see it now, a pair of lacey pink panties hanging from the mirror.

"It looks like a target to me!" Steve declares.

"Steve, seriously, what if someone-" Crip's protest is ignored. Steve whips the solid ball of compacted snow at the Chevette. It whizzes through the opening and shatters the passenger seat window. The outcome, and both visual and audio effects, are the same as before.

"Open in, double out!" Steve shouts, kicking the car as he walks by it, "you two coming?" Steve looks at Crip and Rhonda and throws his hands out, searching for some explanation.

"Why would you do this?" Crip asks.

"Why the fuck not, let's keep going," Steve takes Rhonda's hand, and leads her around the car, "nobody heard a Goddamn thing. We're out in the middle of nowhere." A chorus of barking dogs in the distance disproves Steve's assumption.

"Dogs? Are you fucking kidding me?" Crip shakes his head, "I hate fucking dogs!"

"We better start moving, then. I can see the barn is over across the field," Steve points to the barn across the field.

"What if the dogs are coming from the barn?" Rhonda asks Steve.

"Do you really think I'd suggest going there if I thought the dogs were coming from there? What are you, fucking retarded?" Steve's ability to belittle his wife shined through as his most talented skill, "the two of you are fucking idiots, I swear."

The trio dredges their way across the field of snow. Their legs sink down to the middle of their calves, tripping them up with each step. Crip has the worst time out of them. Halfway to the barn, the barking dogs still in the distance, Crip has had enough.

"You know what?" he pipes up, "I've been thinking about what you said back there, about me being a fucking idiot. And ya know something? You're right. I *am* a fucking idiot, Steve. I'm an idiot for coming along on this bullshit. I'm going back. Fuck this." Crip turns around and stops, "Holy shit. Oh, fuck me."

"What is it now?" Steve turns around with Rhonda. Behind them is a man holding a long rifle and a pair of large, barking dogs attached to leashes, "son of a bitch. Where did he come from?"

"We heard the dogs, dude! He probably heard you smashing out the windows on that fucking car!

And look! He's got a fucking gun! He's gonna shoot us, Steve," Crip says, a look of concern growing on his face.

"He ain't gonna shoot no one, it's just to scare us," Steve says.

"Boys," Rhonda interjects, "he's getting closer. Let's get to the barn! Come on!"

"Okay, whatever you say then. Run!" Steve declares, and the three of them start running as fast as the snowpack allows. The barking grows in volume until it is louder than their struggle through the snowpack. Steve and Rhonda gain ground quicker than Crip, who is losing his battle with the terrain.

"Guys! Wait for me god dammit!" he screams, tears streaming down his face as he trips through the snow. He can feel the dogs getting closer to him as the distance between Steve and Rhonda grows.

They don't ever look back. Not once, he notes to himself, *that son of bitch only cares about himself!* Crip tries to speed it up, but the faster he moves, the more his spastic leg drags through the snow, slowing him down.

"Fuck you, Steve!" Crip gives them the finger. Next to him, a divot of earth and snow blow into the air as the crack of a gun echoes across the field, "Guys! Steve! Rhonda! Help me!" Crip screams.

But they don't look back.

They keep running away, even when the gun

fires a second time. From the moment the bullet hits Crip in the lower back and blows out the front of his groin, he watches Steve and Rhonda run to the barn, not giving a fuck about him.

The impact of the seventy-five caliber musket ball causes Crip to arch his back and freeze in place, paralyzed. The musket ball, with the aid of a powder charge and the magic of kinetic energy, enters the small of his back. It penetrates his pelvic bone and exits the front through his groin with the be-all-end-all of money shots. A spray of blood covers the snow in front of him.

The projectile plows through bone and meat. It transforms Crip's wondrous cock and balls into a visceral display of mangled flesh. Looking down, he sees a giant hole in his pants where his cock used to be and can't believe his eyes.

Gawking at his emasculation, gravity takes hold and pulls Crip to the ground. He faceplants into the snow. A burning fire shoots through his lower back and groin. He tries to push himself up to a knee, but he falls back down when pain surges through his body.

How did I let this some of a bitch talk me into doing this? And now I'm going to fucking die! Crip tells himself.

"Stackhouse! Help! Stackhouse!" he shouts, spitting out a mouthful of bloody snow in the process. The barking of the dogs becomes a cacophony of madness, drowning out his cries and pounding in his head. He drags his body forward with his good arm, plowing the snowpack. It's a futile effort.

"Looks like you missed the *'Trespassers Will Be Shot'* sign back at the junkyard," a man says. His voice is deep and scratchy, an old voice, muffled behind a mask of some sort, "and the beware of dogs sign, too. Wait, there weren't no *'Beware of Dog'* sign. Sorry about that. Um, so I think I best tell ya to beware of dogs. *Kill, Fang!*" The command results in a ferocious growl.

It ends with a hundred and seventy-five-pound Irish wolfhound biting into the back of Crip's neck.

"You ain't from 'round here, are ya? I wasn't from here, but I am now," the crazy old man says, "the god told me so. The god told me you were coming, too. The god knows everything. The god provides."

Crip cries out from the shock rather than the pain. Not much can hurt more than having your dick blown off with a seventy-five-caliber musket ball reach around. The giant dog shakes Crip, causing his head to wobble violently back and forth.

"Pretty soon I'll be joining the rest of the ancestors under the hill," through the chaos, Crip sees flashes of a tall man standing over him. A bronzed wolf mask covers his face. The man is pointing to the big hill they walked around.

"Make a spot for me, would ya? You'll be getting there first," the snow around Crip turns from white to pink and into red. The other dog latches onto his groin and pulls in the opposite direction.

Crip, once known as Dickie Pecker, hears something in his neck snap, and before his brain can understand what has happened to him, his body says, "*fuck this!*" and checks out.

Behind them is a man holding a long rifle and a pair of large, barking dogs attached to leashes.

4

Clad in wool jackets, Jack and Peggy walk hand-in-hand through the rings of white, barren trees. Snow from a recent finger of lake effect sticks to the branches and trunks. The sun hangs above the hilltops, painting them red as it slowly sinks.

Jack carries a spade with a wood shaft in his off hand. Likewise, Peggy's arm is looped through a wicker basket. A bouquet of dried flowers, rose hips and Queen Anne's lace rests within.

The couple comes to a small mountain brook. It runs through their property, down from neighboring Morgan Hill, and ultimately feeds the irrigation line. It's always clean and trickling, except on the coldest days. Today, the sun graced the hilltop, resulting in a fresh current. On its banks, the dried reeds of cattails project through the

snowpack.

Peggy stops and breaks off a handful of reeds.

"These will do," she tells her husband. He nods. It's a silent affirmation for Peggy to start. She twists, pinches, and bends the reeds, weaving them together.

"You're good at this," Jack tells his wife.

"I wish the girls were here, they used to love making the crosses today. They're so good at it."

"The professional students learned from the best, no?"

"That they did, dear, that they did. It's for the best. They don't like being around you on this date. You get too grouchy," she tells her husband. He grumbles and shakes his head. Peggy ignores him and continues talking, "You know, I've been thinking a lot about this lately."

"About what?"

"Look," Peggy points to the gigantic power lines cutting through the state land bordering their property. Crows cover the towers and portions of the lines, "she's always there, watching us, reminding us, isn't she," Peggy didn't ask a question.

"Aye, that she is," Jack says. She stops talking and focuses on the task at hand. He watches her finish weaving the pinwheel of Saint Brigid's cross from the cattail reeds. It's a work of art, as it has been every year they go through with this ritual.

Jack finds a dogberry bush on the creek's side, its white fruit blending in with the snow on the plant's leaves. He strips a handful of the leaves and berries off the bush and puts them in the pocket of his blue and black checkered flannel jacket.

"For the life of me, I still don't know why you were rude to the witch," Peggy says.

"You're going there, now?" he scoffs, "Why is it you are skilled at remembering everything that ever happens?"

"It's part of my job, and it's in the contract."

"Contract?"

"The one you signed when I said, 'I do',"

"Yeah, okay, whatever. I swear that was a hundred years ago."

"I've noticed, in our time on this earth together, regardless of when it did go down, everything happened a hundred years ago with you."

"You're full of epiphanies today. Well, it did! It was forever and a hundred years, however, you want to refer to it. You know I didn't know she was a witch when she asked me to dance. So how is me telling her 'no' being rude?"

"It's all in how you say 'no'," Peggy replies, and walks away from her husband, towards the center of the orchard's rings. Another gunshot rings out, from the distance as she walks away, scaring up a flock of birds from the Mountain Ash.

5

Steve Stackhouse doesn't know if the dogs are eating Crip, but he's pretty sure they are. He really doesn't care. They aren't eating Steve or Rhonda, and at this moment in time, Crip's lethal setback is all that matters. Sure, he feels bad for Crip, but the recently deceased knew the risk of their little venture. And now Dickie Pecker, also known as Crip, owned a new, albeit posthumous, nickname.

Dog Chow.

Mr. and Mrs. Stackhouse run through the snow, putting as much cornfield as they can between them and the crazy man behind them. The barn ahead also means roads, plowed with no snow, and an easy escape from whatever the fuck is going on.

Steve reaches the old, rickety barn first. He collapses on the wall and takes a deep breath. Before he exhales, Rhonda has joined him, exasperated. She digs her phone out of her pocket.

"You think there's a plug in here? Where the fuck are we? East Bumfuck?"

"Pretty much," Steve replies, "plus, I don't see any power lines coming to the barn, so who knows about a plug."

"Is this the barn the weed is in?"

"I sure hope so, otherwise Crip died for nothing."

"This is fucked up. Somebody is going to jail, Steve."

"Well, it ain't gonna be us," he looks over his shoulder.

"You're goddamn right it ain't gonna be us. Crip was right, we shoulda stayed home," Steve ignores his wife. Instead of listening to her, he instead focuses on the man who shot Crip.

The man isn't walking toward them, he's walking back to the junkyard. He has the dogs leashed, and he's dragging something behind him. It's difficult to see, but it's leaving a pink streak in the snow.

Is that what's left of Crip? Steve wonders, *better yet, where the fuck is that guy going?* He surveys the area. Down the driveway from the barn, he can see

Route 11. A small hill, almost a perfect circular mound, rises next to the barn. Over the hill and across another field, he can see a distant residence and a large dairy operation, spread out near the highway. The edge of a barren tree orchard lays behind the barn, the leafless trees are an ominous, skeletal barrier.

Rhonda moves before Steve. She opens a door with a brass knob and enters the barn.

"Hey, bitch, what are you doing, wait for me," Steve joins his wife inside. Rhonda stands with her arms crossed on her chest. Her face is not a picture of happiness. It's quite the opposite.

"Weed? This ain't weed. What the fuck is it, Steve? Cos it ain't fucking weed," Rhonda points to the rafters. Steve turns his eyes to the ceiling and sees dozens of dried sunflowers hanging in the rafters. Each of them an emaciated eye, watching Steve and Rhonda.

"It's sunflowers?"

"I know they're sunflowers, Steven David," Rhonda loved to go full first and middle name on him when she got angry, "so much for your reliable source."

"Fuck you, really, you're going to go there?"

"Where else would I go? And Crip died for this? For nothing?"

The bay doors at the other side of the barn swing open, startling the duo and revealing the man with the rifle, pointing the weapon at them. He blocks their way to the driveway and route 80.

"Your friend didn't die for nothing, missy, his sacrifice is honored by the god," he says, the words muffled, his face obscured by a bronzed wolf mask. Steve knows the musket he's pointing at them only has one ball stuffed in its barrel.

"*The* god?" Steve asks the masked man, stepping back to the door he and Rhonda entered the barn though.

"Aye, the god of the mound. I have the god's holy mark," the man holds the musket with one hand and rips open his jacket with the other, revealing a deep blue triskelion tattoo on his chest, "ya see? I was chosen, oh so many years ago, yes, I was. You two? You're chosen, too, but not for this mark."

"You're crazy, man, fucking crazy all this talk about gods and shit. Why did you kill Crip? Fuck you, man!" Steve can sense the opening behind him and knows the window of opportunity to run is closing.

"The god's sleeping, now, with it being winter and the cold and all. But it'll wake up when the flowers bloom, hungry. And it won't care if your bodies started to rot after thawing."

"Oh, fuck you, crazy man, we're out of here," Steve dismisses the old man and tugs at Rhonda's arm, "come on, we have to go, now!" Steve bolts out the open door, pulling Rhonda along. They run toward the tree orchard.

The man walks through the barn and out the door with no rush. As he takes his time, he watches Steve and Rhonda run away. He gets a feel for their gait as any good hunter would. He aims the musket at the pair.

"Fuck me? Oh no, young man, that's not how this works. You can run away all you like, we'll still getcha. The god provides," he squeezes the trigger.

The hammer of the musket trips forward and strikes a patch of flint with a crack of thunder. The resulting spark ignites a charge of black powder. The combustion within a confined space sends a seventy-five-caliber ball of lead soaring down a forty-six-inch-long barrel at eighteen hundred feet per second.

A burst of fire and a cloud of smoke herald the projectile's imminent arrival. With the grace of a champion, it comes from behind in true underdog fashion and smacks its target in the back of the head.

Steve happens to be looking at Rhonda when the musket shot hits her. In one breath she is running with him, a handheld over her mouth in an effort to mute herself from screaming.

In the next her face and hand explode, the fingers pinwheeling through the air.

Steve saw something like this once in an old movie, that Civil War one with Denzel Washington and Matthew Broderick, Glory was its name. Steve loved Civil War stuff. He hero-worshipped Robert E. Lee and would wear a Confederate flag if he wanted to.

It's history! he would argue. despite being a Ninth-grade drop-out with a complete lack of knowledge regarding actual historical events. Near the beginning of the movie, some guy is marching in formation next to Matthew Broderick, *and his head fucking explodes when a cannonball hits it.*

It doesn't take a cannonball to blow Rhonda Stackhouse's jaw, teeth, tongue, sinus cavity, and cheekbones out like candy from a blood and pus-filled piñata. A seventy-five-caliber musket ball does fine all on its own.

The crack of the flintlock rifle follows, echoing through the orchard. Rhonda's body falls to the ground and rolls on her back. Under her eyes is a gaping red and black void where the bottom of her face once used to be.

Horrified, Steve still can't help but notice the line where Rhonda's makeup ends.

He gives the man in the wolf mask the finger and runs off, deeper into the orchard.

6

A trio of standing stones, brought to the farm long before men recorded such transactions, form a henge at the orchard's epicenter. The weathered slate monoliths encircle an altar slab cut from limestone, all of it covered in fresh snow. Faded pictograms, scratched into the surface ages before, remember stories and deeds. Some are long forgotten.

Some can never be.

Next to the shortest of the stones is a Celtic cross, carved from red granite. Peggy wipes the snow off the altar slab with her sleeve, sets the basket on the cold stone, and clears off the cross.

She stops to catch her breath as the words carved into the monument are revealed.

In loving memory
CONNER CULLHAIN MAC TÍRE

Jack places a hand on his wife's shoulder. She grasps it, then leans her cheek into her husband's forearm.

"I'm sorry, Peggy, so sorry," Jack says, stifling tears of his own.

"I know you are," she sniffles, then pats his hand and stands, "come on. We've got work to do before the sun sets," Peggy steps aside to the altar. Without speaking, Jack drives the spade into the earth at the foot of the gravestone.

He digs while Peggy stares at the pictograms and Ogham runes etched into the standing stones. They tell an ancient myth of a mighty warrior, driven mad by the moon, who devours the sun. To some, it's a common mythological archetype used to explain the days and seasons. The McEntire clan has a far more intimate relationship with this fable.

She reads the Ogham and, in her head, reads the folk poem in the old tongue...

Cú dílis duit a bheith.
Riamh dílis don lámh a bheathaíonn.
Féachfaidh mac na talún sibh sa tsúil.

Riamh madraí macánta, buile nach bréag.

And then, she recites it aloud, in English,

"A loyal cur ye be.
Ever faithful to the hand that feeds.
Son of the land'll look ye' in the eye.
Ever honest, mad dogs don't lie."

Peggy speaks the last word as Jack strikes wood with the spade's blade. She smiles and gathers the woven cross and dried flowers as her husband continues to dig and uncover their hidden treasure.

"Almost there," Jack says, throwing shovels full of dirt out of the long, deep hole he dug. His head is all Peggy can see above the dirt-covered snow.

"I never told you Emmy came to the cottage," Peggy says, "after you told her to, um, put her clothes on and, uh, feck off. She stood on the stoop, red with anger, pulling her hair out in clumps, spitting at me."

The revelation is a bombshell. Jack stops digging. Peggy hears the shovel fall, the metal handle clanging on the wood. A scowl grows on her husband's face.

"Is that so? You wait a hundred fecking years to casually spring this on me?"

"It wasn't a hundred years ago," she smiles and shakes her head, "but yeah, she did. When she showed up at the door, I told her she wasn't welcome there. She didn't care, she went on and on about me and you and what could I do for you that she couldn't. I let her vent, then I closed the door on her face."

"I would hope so. And why are you just telling me this now?"

"I think you should know. She begged me to give you to her. Told me how she needed you and your blood. And how you refused her."

"And you wondered why I told Emmy no when she asked me to dance? I take no chances with a damned witch like her. Am I wrong? Look what she did anyhow."

"I never questioned your fidelity, husband. The point is, I was nice to her that day when she came begging for you. You should have been nice to her at the May Pole, but I understand why you didn't. It's why I forgave you for all of this," she points to the standing stones, "it's why the girls forgave you because it wasn't your fault, it was all a jealous-"

"Witch?"

"Yes, but it's how we came to," she stops to gather her thoughts, shaking her head and biting her bottom lip, "the girls, they were with me that day. I told them to stay away from Emmy, we got no business messing with her, and we ain't ever gonna have none. So, you just leave her be, and she leaves us be."

"As you should've."

"And then she goes and makes me out to be a liar."

"I'm sorry. I let you down," Jack bows his head in shame.

"Oh, feck you, and your sorries over this, Jack," Peggy flips her husband the finger, "I'm not blaming you. I'm just venting. I love you. Let's get this done. I need a drink."

"Me, too," Jack returns to his labor and in a matter of minutes, he pushes a small casket out of the hole, "can you give me a hand?" He asks his wife. She reaches down into the grave and helps her husband out. He brushes the dirt off his jacket and follows up with a kick to the casket. It slides in the snow and bangs off the altar slab.

"Aw, shit," he slips.

"Jack!" Peggy admonishes her husband, "have some respect! Be-"

"Be nice?" he interrupts her, "yeah, I know," he laughs as he speaks and shakes his head.

"Yes, really," she grasps a handful of the dried flowers in her hand, "Open it, please," she directs her husband. Jack obliges, using the spade's blade as a crowbar. Long iron nails, the heads aged with rust, squeal as they pop out of the wood. Jack rips the cover of the coffin off and throws it aside by the pile of dirt. A whiff of decay blows out of the casket.

7

Steve cuts into the orchard through a gap between trees. Wild rose bushes weave through the trees. Some animal, likely a deer, braved the thorns and partially cleared out a bush while filling its belly. As fate would have it, today Steve Stackhouse uses this as a doorway to sanctuary. The remaining thorns rip through the nylon shell of his jacket, pulling out strands of insulation, and scratch the exposed flesh on his hands and face, drawing lines of blood.

Once through the barrier, he curses and adjusts the dew rag on his head before dashing down the lane of the orchard between rows of trees. Fear prevents him from stopping and making himself a target for the dude in the wolf mask.

The orchard is almost a maze, running in a

spiral of circles with a stream following along. The snow isn't deep here, and it allows him to move faster. He comes upon a stream and finds fresh tracks in the snow.

People? he asks himself. He looks behind, sees there's no sign of his pursuer, and sighs in relief. The presence of people means help. *Maybe someone has a working cell phone and can call for help.*

Steve follows the tracks.

•

Jack holds the coffin in his arms. Inside is the nude, emaciated body of a crone. Her skin is wrinkled and dry, and long, white hairs lay about a bald head, creating a silver halo. The wretched thing is bound in thorny vines and covered in dried flowers and the familiar pinwheels of St. Brigid's Cross. One of her eyes is missing, a black hole in her shriveled skull. The other, clouded with glaucoma, stares blankly. Stuffed in her mouth is a handkerchief filled with rose hips.

"Well, if it isn't the bitch in a box," Jack says, leaning on his shovel's handle. The crone's cheek twitches, and her eye moves. Peggy reaches down and pulls the handkerchief out of the woman's mouth. Rose hips spill out, adding to the dried vegetation in the box.

"Jack, what did I say about being nice?" Peggy

corrects her husband. He shrugs his shoulders. A dry, rasping noise comes from the wretched thing in the coffin. It spits out a mouthful of dust and dirt.

"Ah, the cur and his fae bitch return to torture me anew," the crone cackles, her mouth now free to speak. Bits of dried flowers continue to spit out of the crone's mouth with each of her words. "End me!" she demands.

"As long as we live, Emmy, so shall you," Jack tells his captive.

"So ye believe, Sean Chulainn Mac Tíre," the witch's cloudy eye seems to look straight through him when she speaks. Jack winces at a name he hasn't heard in ages, "I listen to thee from below, I see thee from above. I heard yer words as ye dug me up. The god's curse ye've not yet escaped."

"Curse? You mean our blessing?" Peggy interjects.

"Look at ye, with yer faithful lapdog, stolen from me by a changeling harlot," the hag taunts the McEntire matriarch. Peggy ignores the comment, but Emmy doesn't stop running her toothless mouth, "one day they'll find ye and find me, and release me."

"They?" Jack blinks, smirks, and shakes his head, "no one seeks your bag of bones this dog has buried in his backyard. And if, by chance, someone or something does? They won't find you in this forest of witchwood."

"Listen to thee, mocking me when I'm helpless in this prison. I bet ye miss yer son, I bet both thee miss yer little boy when the Bealtaine fires burn bright," the crone taunts Peggy, "I can see the other side. He's not there, cos he lost his soul to the-!" Jack punches the crone in the face. Her head bangs into the wood of her coffin and a cloud of dust billows out. She coughs and gags.

"Feck you," Peggy says and spits on Emmy. The witch laughs and hacks up a bit of muddy phlegm to spit back, but it drools down her leathery chin. Peggy's tone remains firm, "you're in no position to be talking any shit, Emmy."

"So much for being nice, hah?" Jack adds and winks at his wife. She purses her lips and furrows her brow in response.

"I'll see thee in Hell, dogs!"

"No, no, Emmy. This is where you're wrong. This? Right here and now? This is Hell. And us? We're the fecking Devil. You'll pay for your sins against our clan for long as we live. And we plan to live for a bit."

•

Steve rounds a curve and stops. Ahead of him is an unexpected sight. A trio of stones surrounds an altar. And standing at the base of one of the stones, next to a pile of dirt, are a man and a woman, holding a small box. They drop it into a hole in the ground.

Is that a coffin? What did I stumble onto? A pet funeral or something?

The woman looks up from her business and sees Steve. He starts screaming to them, his words running into themselves. They look at him with expressions of surprise and confusion. Steve stops and slows down his words.

"There's a crazy motherfucker in a wolf mask with a musket and man-eating dogs chasing me! He just killed my best friend and my wife!" Steve manages to get out in a single breath.

"Slow down, son, you're going to have a heart attack," the man says. Steve approaches them, stopping when he's socially distant.

"I'm sorry, I'm so sorry to bother you. Please do you have a cell phone? We need to call the police. There's a crazy man chasing me!"

"There, there. We've been waiting for you," the woman says to Steve. His spine turns numb.

"You don't understand. There's a man chasing me with a gun!"

"Yes, we have," the man says, "the god provides."

What did they just say? They've been waiting?

"The god provides," the man repeats the woman's phrase like it's scripture. But it's no scripture Steve's heard before. The crack of a rifle interrupts his train of thought. The shot hits Steve in the back of the neck, making it impossible for him to speak and preventing him from screaming out in shock. This is typical when your larynx has been removed by a musket ball. Instead of words, blood spits out of his mouth and a three-inch diameter hole in his neck, completing a sentence of frothy gurgles.

"Dinner time, bitch," the man says, he reaches into Steve's pocket, removes his cell phone, and pushes Stackhouse's teetering body into the grave.

Dinner time? He ponders as he falls, then Steve Stackhouse sees what awaits him.

A visage of hell is the last thing he ever sees.

•

Jack helps the wounded man along, but not before retrieving his cell phone. He pushes him into Emmy's grave and steps back.

The blood gushing from Steve's gunshot wound lands on the witch's husk first. The dried flesh sucks it in, bringing about an instant transformation.

Her body morphs into a hairless, chimeric amalgam of Emmy and a canine. Long, wicked teeth line the thing's maw. It bites down onto Steve's head, crunching through the bone, devouring it. Goops of cranial matter squish out between its lips.

The mouth opens and closes, sending bits and pieces of Steve into the air. Most of Steve's blood is gone at this point, it's either on the ground or absorbed into whatever Emmy has become.

In less than two minutes, Emmy devours Steve Stackhouse, from his head down to the soles of his boots. Jack and Peggy turn their heads, preferring not to witness the feeding.

"I'm glad that's done," Jack says when it's over.

"Me, too," Peggy confirms, whipping a bit of Steve off her sleeve, "You got some in your beard," she points out to her husband. He feels around and flicks it off.

"Everything okay now?" The man in the wolf mask steps out from behind the skeleton of an apple tree. Smoke still rises from the barrel of his musket.

"Hi, Uncle Rory. Good shot," Jack says to their friend and neighbor.

"It's my pleasure," the man in the wolf mask replies, "I learned from the best."

"That you did," Jack says, smiling.

"Thanks for calling us earlier," Peggy adds, "you're right, he was perfect. It's funny ya know, funny weird, how the god provides us with exactly what we need."

"That's why it's a god, for feck's sake," Jack says, "here's his phone, we don't need it pinging off when the powers that be go looking for them." Rory takes the phone from Jack.

"I'll see that it ends up in Syracuse with the other phones. I've got to go to the state park and get their car, too. Ya need any help with this?" Rory asks.

"Naw, we've got it from here, old friend."

"Old is right, I feel like I've known you for a hundred years."

"It seems that way, doesn't it?"

"It sure does," Rory replies, then adds, "the god provides," before he walks away, leaving Jack and Peggy alone with the thing in the box, still chewing on bits of Steve Stackhouse.

The thing shifts back, returning to its former state, albeit now a bit less dried out after soaking up Steve's blood. Emmy licks her lips and smacks her toothless gums.

"More, give me more!" the witch croaks, blood dripping off her lips. Jack empties his pocket of dogberries into the coffin. They fall on the woman's body, paralyzing her for a moment, allowing Jack a window of opportunity.

"I don't think so," Jack says and pushes her back into the coffin. He grabs Emmy's lower jaw, and holds it firm. Peggy retrieves a small knife from her jacket. The berries roll off the body, and Emmy thrashes and squirms. It doesn't help her, she's unable to break her restraints. Peggy kneels next to the box with the knife in hand.

"Hold her still, Jackie," Peggy, tells her husband.

"What does it look like I'm doing, for feck's sake," Jack pushes her down and uses the coffin to aid him. It works.

Emmy tries to speak but can't make words without the use of her lower jaw. The resulting gibberish is a crackling noise. The McEntire clan's matron solves the problem for her captive altogether. With a flick of her wrist, Peggy's knife snips off Emmy's tongue and throws it aside, into the snow. A stream of black blood squirts out of the crone's toothless maw.

"Give me the jerky from the hunt," Peggy orders her husband. He complies, pulling it out of another pocket.

"That should do it for another year," she says and stuffs the handkerchief, refilled with the jerky and fresh rose hips, back in Emmy's mouth, stopping the leak.

A muffled, howling screech grows from Emmy. Her cry, too, becomes trapped inside the coffin when Jack slams the lid back down. He hammers the nails in with the spade and slides the coffin back into its grave. It lands with a thud on the frozen ground. They can hear Emmy's wailing until the final shovel of dirt lands on the grave, as the last light of day concedes to the darkness.

"It's finished," Jack says to his wife.

"It is," she replies, "let's go home and sit by the fire."

"I'd like that. Conner used to love sitting by the fire on his birthday, too."

"Yes, he did."

"Do you think Erin might join us? Maybe we could face time with Rosie?"

"I think that could all be arranged," Peggy McEntire says, takes her husband's hand, and together, they walk home.

•

The birds wait for Jack and Peggy to be out of sight before swarming down on black wings, drawn to the carrion. The crows engulf the monuments. They feast on the remaining scraps of Steve Stackhouse and their mistress's tongue. Some bring their own meals to share. A large crow lands on the head stone and drops an offering to its mistress under the earth, a human finger.

A silver ring set with a small ruby still rests near the severed digit's third knuckle. The gemstone captures the last light of the twilight and flickers as the wail of a banshee builds. It grows from the grave, rolls over the hills of snow, and blends into the wind as the night brings close to another midwinter's day.

ST ROOSTER BOOKS

THE GOD PROVIDES - 118 - THOMAS R CLARK

ST ROOSTER BOOKS

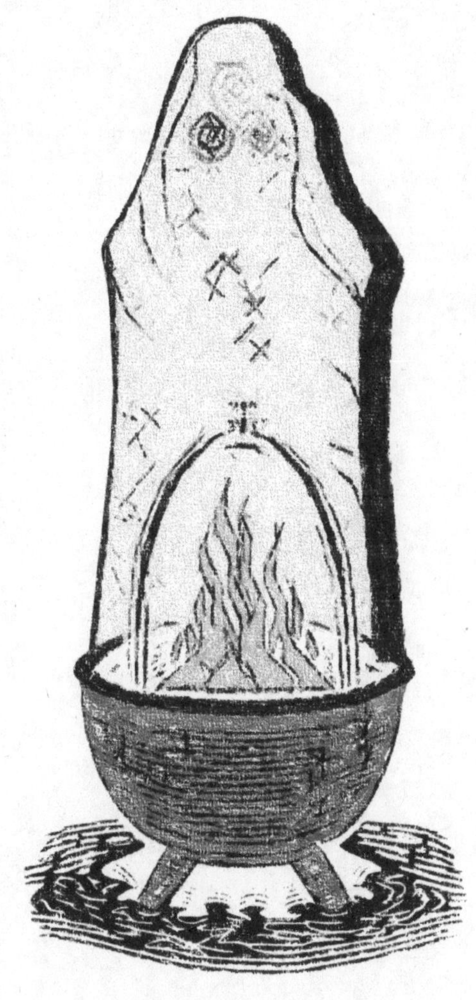

ST ROOSTER BOOKS

ST ROOSTER BOOKS

AN IRISH MYTH?

There was a time, long ago, before the Gaels and the Celts came to Eire. In this era, the Picts called Muicinis their home. The painted people, tattooed with spirals of woad, tilled the land and forged legends.

The greatest warrior of yore, Cú Mac Cullhain, sat upon the throne of Inis Fáil alongside his shield maiden and queen, Éimear. She bore him a son, Conchobhar, and two daughters, Éirinn and Rowan.

He wielded the magical sword Cúcholg, the Wolf Cleaver, bequeathed unto him by the serpent god of the bale fires, Crom Cruach. The great blade could smite mountains and struck fear into the enemies of Inis Fáil.

With the legendary Grand Arch Druid, the Myrddyn as his chief advisor, Mac Cullhain ruled as a fair and benevolent king. The peoples of the Emerald Isle saw prosperity and peace. Until the Formorians came.

Led by Balor One-Eye, the barbarians sailed in dragon ships from across the northern sea. At first, they raided the coast, striking random fishing villages at random, killing the men, raping the women, and fleeing before the king's soldiers could engage.

Their greed grew bolder with each raid, moving further inland, until they stole Mac Cullhain's personal cattle. The furious king, fed up with the Formorians, gathered an army of his fiercest men, and struck out to retrieve his prize herd.

The Mórrígan, Goddess of War and Queen of Banshees, sought to aid Mac Cullhain in his quest. The gods are fickle, and they seldom make an offer without asking for some payment in advance. Thus, The Phantom Queen came to Mac Cullhain in the night, as he prepared for bed.

"Lay with me and know me, and I will steal the wind from Balor One-Eye's sails and trap him for you," The Mórrígan told Cú Mac Cullhain. Ever faithful to the mother of his children, the king resisted the goddess's advances.

"I have sworn the same fealty to my queen as the people of Inis Fáil have to my throne," he declared, and cast The Mórrígan from his bed.

"How dare you say no to me, the Phantom Queen!" Furious at being rejected, The Mórrígan screamed a curse upon Mac Cullhain. "Ríastrad cú dílis duit!" she screeched, "Riamh dílis don lámh a bheathaíonn," each word pierced Mac Cullhain's being, "Mac na talún beidh cuma ye 'sa tsúil," a palsy overtook the king, "Riamh madraí macánta, buile nach bréag." The goddess transformed into a flock of ravens and flew away.

Inside his tent, anger filled Mac Cullhain with spasms of rage. He tore off his clothing and ran into the night. High in the sky, the crimson star of the war goddess twinkled, calling to Mac Cullhain to embrace her.

He would not spurn her a second time. The Mórrígan's curse gripped the king, twisting and wrenching him, changing him from a man into the beast of his namesake. The wolf who was once a king howled to his Phantom Queen.

Mac Cullhain's son heard the clamor and came rushing out of his tent. Fearing the beast ate the king, Conchobhar drew his father's sword, Cúcholg, and attacked the monster. He swung the great sword and missed. The creature leaped on Conchobhar Mac Cullhain and devoured him.

After filling its belly, the monster fell asleep. The soldiers surrounding the incident stared in shock as the wolf creature reverted to its natural form ... their king, Cú Mac Cullhain.

Coming to his own senses, the king wept, and a great melancholy spread across Inis Fáil. To spite The Mórrígan, he lit balefires across the countryside and pursued the army of Balor One-Eye through day and night, until he made them pay for his son's death with steel, bone, and flesh.

And so, the great king of Inis Fáil, Cú Mac Cullhain, cursed to go wolfing by the Mórrígan's War Spasm, wandered the countryside in mourning. Fearing he would eat his daughters and wife, Mac Cullhain sought the wisdom of his most trusted advisor, the Myrddyn, to break the curse.

"The curses of gods are beyond the capabilities of mortals," the Myrddyn told the king, "Ye must find the secret of how to turn the curse into a blessing. Only then can your family survive."

"Where can I learn this secret?" Cú Mac Cullhain demanded of the Myrddyn.

"From another god, of course. But know ye well, the price to pay for this secret be high."

The king dealt with the fickle gods of Inis Fáil on more than one occasion. Long ago, Crom Cruach bestowed upon Mac Cullhain his great sword, Cúcholg, the Wolf Cleaver. So now, the king returned to the well from which the God of Plenty resided.

"What is it ye ask of me, Cú Mac Cullhain? Long have ye been faithful to thy bride. Long have ye been faithful to thy crown. And long have ye been faithful to Crom Cruach," the god spoke from its lair deep within the Earth.

"The secret to removing The Mórrígan's curse of ríastrad from my blood."

"Curse?" Crom Cruach said, "Ye are not cursed, ye are blessed by the ríastrad."

"How can this be a blessing? I have devoured my only son. Now I fear I may do the same to my wife and daughters," the king pleaded to his god.

"Thy family shalt blessed be to go wolfing with thee. Take thy kin and thy leave with the gods, to the hills across the waves. Forever honor Crom Cruach with balefire and family."

Crom Cruach bid Mac Cullhain his leave. He would return to the well on this day, when the balefires burned, to fulfill his part of the bargain.

Never Forget ... the god provides.

ST ROOSTER BOOKS

3 BEALTAINE

THE GOD IN THE WELL

ST ROOSTER BOOKS

THE GOD IN THE WELL

(Featuring the poetry of James Matthew Byers)

1

Summer comes to the Foothills a month before the rest of New York. Freed from the grip of winter, the days grow with the flora. The sun shines, providing the leaves the necessary light to flourish. Lush greenery grows overnight, fed by the cold rains of spring. A unique aroma permeates the air, a combination of cow shit and flowering corn.

Orchards and vineyards line the hillsides between swaths of forest. In the flatlands of the hill valleys, crop fields and dairy cow pastures take up most of the real estate. The farmers sow their seeds and tend the herds, bees pollinate apple blossoms, and the wineries tend to their grapes.

Homesteads sit close to the main highways traversing the region. State Routes 5 & 20, 80, 11, and 13 are the most traveled. These roads weave through hamlets, such as Tinker's Falls, and villages, the likes of LaFayette or Cazenovia.

Travelers, city folk from Syracuse and Binghamton being the most common, use these highways. They take Sunday drives or to visit the region's agricultural attractions. Still others are simply passing through.

Take Andrew, aka Andy, Rivers for example. Hitchhiking across New York through apple country seemed like a good idea when the recent high school graduate planned the excursion. With no collegiate plans set in stone, what else is there for him to do?

Armored in denim and cotton with a pair of Levi's and an AC/DC T-shirt, Andy's trusty Chuck Converses carried him out on his walkabout. With no endgame planned, his final destination promised to remain a mystery until he arrived.

The young man believed himself indestructible, a shared hubris of every teen-age white kid in 1984 America. An only child with a single parent who barely acknowledged his existence, Andy liked to push things to the limits. Sure, hitching is ill-advised at best, but Andy fancied himself a bit of a danger addict.

Like most kids his age, he's dead fucking wrong about everything.

•

Somewhere between New Woodstock and Apulia, Andy sees the Chevette. Something doesn't look right about the guy driving the subcompact. The little blue hatchback drives past Andy in the opposite lane on Route 20. The driver brakes so hard the tires squeal and burn tracks on the pavement. Andy doesn't have to look to know the car does a three-point turn in the road. Nobody is ever this eager to pick up a lone hitchhiker.

He's coming for me, Andy's sense of self-preservation whispers.

The car pulls up alongside, substantiating Andy's paranoia. Anxiety pounds his heart with the force of a hammer. Rust borders the car's wheel wells. He can smell burning oil and hear a slight ticking in the engine's pattern.

The Bad man is Overweight, and middle-aged, with more than a hint of pattern baldness and a stereotypical mustache. He stares at Andy through black rimmed glasses. He huffs and puffs as he rolls down the passenger's window, unveiling a pungent odor. A pink thong hangs from the rearview mirror. This omen is all the warning Andy needs. When the Bad Man opens his mouth to speak it's the starting gun of race.

"Hey, buddy. You looking to get laid?" the Bad Man says, a giant grin on his face. Andy isn't sure what bothers him more. The motherfucker's immediate cut to the chase or the disturbing confidence in his voice. Andy can feel this isn't the Bad Man's first time picking up a hitcher.

Fight or flight hormones take over. Andy chooses the former and runs from the roadside. He jumps the ditch between the shoulder and the property line. His feet sink to his ankles in the mud on the other side, but he pulls them out and runs. The field stretches out before him.

"Wait! Why are you running? I can give you a ride!" He hears the door of the car close as the Bad Man shouts after him.

Fuck you. Andy's mind forms the words, but they never come out. Instead, he propels his body forward, navigating the unstable terrain, putting as much real estate as he can between himself and the Bad Man. He looks over his shoulder, hoping the Bad Man went back to his car and is driving away.

Disappointment greets his optimism.

How is this fat piece of shit running? Why can't he have a fucking heart attack and die? he thinks, wishing for this or any other measure of bad luck to fall upon the Bad Man. *Why couldn't it be thunder storming? Then an errant lightning bolt could ...*

Andy passes a grove of tall trees, revealing a

blue farmhouse set near the top of a small hill, hidden behind a swatch of birch and box maples. Its windows are shuttered, with wreathes of yellow flowers hanging on each. He could find help here, a place to hide, or maybe find something to fend this fucking sicko off.

The field of mud stops at a man-made curb, made from concrete. It separates the muck from a lawn. The beveled surface of the barrier is scratched with a pattern of parallel lines. To Andy it might be some form of writing, or someone's kitty went catnip berserk on the cement as it dried. Right now, he doesn't care. His concern is finding safety.

He reaches the residence. The windows are shutters and locked. It appears deserted. He runs behind the home and finds a dilapidated barn. Red flakes of paint, dirty and gray, hang onto water damaged wood in patches. Andy finds a door on rusted hinges. He jerks it with the rusty knob, but it refuses to budge.

The labored panting of his pursuer grows in volume as he continues to gain ground. The longer Andy fucks around with the door, the less time he gives himself to find a weapon.

The hitchhiker goes to the back of the building, putting the barn between him and the Bad Man, giving Andy a brief sense of security. It allows him to gather his thoughts and think of a way out of this without dying or whatever this sick fuck planned for him.

A collapsed door next to the barn lay in pieces. On top of a small hill, a well with its canopy still intact, sits between the structures. The yellow paint on the wood is faded and peeling. A dozen jagged, miss-cut slate slabs encircle the well. Standing about a yard apart, they vary in width and height, the tallest is about six feet high.

Andy sees a pitchfork sticking into the ground, next to the door. His hopes of getting out of this alive raises a notch.

"Thank you, baby Jesus!" he screams and runs for the farming tool. Andy gets within a yard of it when the day's bad luck slaps him in the face, again. This time, his foot finds a dead tree root, poking up through the wet grass. The resulting trip sends him flailing to the ground with all expenses paid.

Andy face-plants at the base of a short standing stone. Stars of pain fill the blackness inside his eyes. He bites his tongue and lip and can taste the blood swelling in his mouth. Stunned, the teenager stands up and shakes his head.

He sees the pitchfork is within reach. He grasps its worn, wooden handle with both hands, and swings around. Slivers roll off under his fingertips as he holds the makeshift weapon at the ready.

The Bad Man is nowhere to be seen. Andy lets out a sigh of relief but doesn't let his guard down.

He can think of no reason why the Bad Man would give up his quarry. He doubts the predator is afraid of the pitchfork.

You better watch it, buddy, I'm armed, whoopsie doo! Andy makes his way to the well, leaning on the side of caution as he goes. A three-foot-tall stone and cement wall circles the well's brick-lined shaft, with a pointed roof housing a winch standing over it. The bucket is long gone, and no rope or chain is attached to the winch.

The air from the well is stale and brackish. Andy wrinkles his nose at the stench. The shaft appears to be endless, a black void of nothing.

How deep is it? Andy muses. He bends down to pick us a stone to drop in and sees the fresh footprint of a large sneaker is depressed into the mud. Andy stands up and steps back, startled at the discovery. Then he jumps a second time, right into his pursuer.

"Got you!" The Bad Man says as he bursts out from behind a standing stone. He grabs Andy with a pair of ham fists, knocking the pitchfork out of his hands.

It falls down the well, the clatter of it bouncing off the brick lining of the shaft. The banging of metal and wood against stone is answered by faint chittering from deep within the well.

The Bad Man's grip is an iron vice. Andy punches at his arms as he squirms, trying to break free. His attempts are useless. He kicks, but his feet slam into the well's rocky exterior.

"Let me go!" Andy screams and screams for help. He doubts anyone would hear, but he screams regardless. A hand comes up to cover his mouth. Andy bites down hard on a pudgy finger.

The Bad Man retaliates, grabbing Andy by the throat. He grunts and squeezes his hand around the hitchhiker's neck, choking Andy in his grip. Instead of crushing his windpipe, he throws the teenager to the ground. Andy's head bangs into the rock wall of the well.

Bursts of white light fill his vision. Andy can't move. The Bad Man stands over him, shaking in anticipation as he undoes the belt holding his slacks up. The pants drop to his knees and his erect cock flicks out to attention.

At least Andy thinks it's a cock. About four inches long, the tip of the thing resembles a snake's forked tongue. The engorged member is deformed, split down the middle of the frenulum and bent to the left at a hard angle.

The Bad Man thrusts his pelvis forward. The twisted phallus throbs and drips a viscous, snot-like emission. The goo puddles in the mud.

"You don't have to be gay to put it in your mouth. I know you want to get laid, buddy!" Andy closes his eyes and throws his arms over his face, "open up!" the Bad Man orders.

"Stay away from me, you son of a-"

A great, chittering roar erupts, piercing Andy's ears, and vibrating through the ground. A sharp crack, as if a tree limb broke in half, follows. The Bad Man, Andy thinks it's the Bad Man, screams- *No, he squeals!*

Something solid slams Andy in the head. He falls backward onto his ass, away from the Bad Man. The teenager moves his arms, opens his eyes, and sees-*The Bad Man's feet falling down the well?*

The booted feet disappear. A vile, snapping and crunching forms the percussion section for a wailing screech echoing up from the depths of the shaft.

"Oh my God!" his tongue trips over his words, "thank you Jesus! Thank you, thank you, thank you Jesus!" Andy falls to his knees, holding his hands in prayer.

Did this just happen? He asks himself, *did this motherfucker just fall down the fucking well? Did something work in my favor for once?*

A pair of headlights dance down a service road alongside a knoll separating even rows of trees. Andy can't believe his streak of good fortune.

Help is coming!

He feels the relief and elation, but his body shakes. His throat is bruised from being choked, and throbs in pain with the absence of adrenaline in his veins. The teenager passes out from exhaustion and shock, his body lying in a clump at the base of the well.

ST ROOSTER BOOKS

2

The late afternoon sun beats down through a window. The brilliant glare wakes Andy from his slumber. He lays in a comfortable bed, covered in clean linens. A lump and a rash on his forehead are a reminder of his brush with the Bad Man.

Where the fuck am I?

Andy looks about, he sees his clothing on a small stand next to the bed. It is washed and folded.

"Hello. I knew ya'd wake up sooner than later," the girl sitting at the end of the bed says, scaring Andy half to death in the process. She's wearing a blue sundress, her long, dark hair pulled back in a ponytail. Andy makes contact with her hazel eyes.

She's beautiful, he tells himself, before asking her, "uh, who are you and where am I?"

"I'm Heather Brannigan. Yer in our guest room.

We found ya outside by the well. Who are ya, what are ya doing here?"

"Um, hi? I'm Andy, Andy Rivers. How did I get here?" he asks, realizing he's naked in a stranger's bed.

And she put him there.

"I asked ya that, and I already told ya we found ya outside at the well, me and my Ma and Pa. Ya looked to be in rough shape. We brought yer car down here to the barn. We didn't snoop, but it has-" she pauses but before she can continue, Andy cuts her off.

"It's not my car. It belongs to some freak who chased me down here, trying to kill me," *or more*, he keeps to himself. "He was some big, weird psychopath who liked to do bad things to … people."

"I like to do bad things to boys," she winks at Andy, then fakes a frown, "I guess this means you don't like pink, lacey thongs. Or maybe you do?" she raises an eyebrow and smirks, "what happened to the guy who chased you?"

"I don't know. He fell into your well? I guess?"

"What do ya mean, *ya guess*? Either he did or he didn't."

"I'm pretty sure he did. I closed my eyes and I heard him trip into the well or something, I'm not totally sure. When I opened my eyes, I saw his feet dropping down into it," *and I heard sounds like something was eating him*, Andy decides to keep this assumption to himself.

"Okay, then. I guess we'll check in the well for a dead creeper. How's yer head feeling?"

"Not too bad."

"That's good. I washed your clothes, cleaned you up," Heather winks at Andy, again, "is there anyone ya might want to call, let 'em know what happened to ya? Let 'em know yer alright and such. Yer folks or maybe yer girlfriend or wife?"

"I'm single, no girlfriend. I'd say my Mom, but she wouldn't be home to answer the phone," an epiphany dawns on Andy, and in this moment, he realizes he's truly alone in life. *I don't have anybody do I? Not a fucking person to fall back on, no family. Not a Goddamn thing.*

"You must be lonely," Heather says, "we're getting ready to go to the Field Days, if yer feeling up to it, ya can join us. Pa was worried ya might be a creeper, but now we know better."

"Field Days?"

"Yeah, the Field Days. Don't they have them where yer from?" Andy shakes his head, all of this is new to him, "Bealtaine, the beginning of summer, some people call it May Day," she announces with glee, "it's a carnival with food and rides and music and," she wiggles her eyebrows, "dancing. You'll have a great time! Tell me you want to come."

"Yeah, sure, I'll come, why not," Andy answers, knowing he could use something to help him forget the incident earlier. He still couldn't believe he escaped a near death experience with a serial rapist.

"We have a saying down here, the god provides, and I'll tell, ain't that the truth! I'm so excited. Okay, ya hafta get ready now, cos we're leaving soon. Gotta beat the sun set. I'll let ya be while ya get dressed. Even though it's not like I don't know what yer packing under the sheets."

"The god provides, hah?" Andy asks.

"Ayup, the god provides," she pats his leg, hops off the bed, and with a curtsy, leaves the room.

3

Dusk nears and the Brannigans, along with their ward, pile into Heather's father's pick-up truck. The teenagers sit in the open bed, leaving her parents, Rory and Joanne, alone in the cab. Heather holds Andy's hand during the ride to the carnival field.

Joanne's attire matches her daughter's. A simple blue sundress. The Brannigan matron is tall and thin. Her blonde locks now platinum as middle-age sets in, tied back with a torc of yellow flowers. Rory's temples and goatee match his wife's tresses, but his head still holds onto the deep black he shares with his daughter.

The ride takes them through spidering back roads. As the sun fades, the Bealtaine fires burn at dusk, lighting the hillsides for the residents of the valley celebrating the start of summer.

The sounds and smells of the festival reach them before Andy sees the spectacle. The LaFayette VFDs practice field is filled with carnival rides and the alluring aromas of fair food. Neon lights create a blue halo over the midway.

"Ya kids have fun now, ya hear? We'll meet back here at 10:00," Rory says to his daughter and her new companion, "and behave," he adds with a wink.

"Come on, follow me!" Heather tells Andy. The girl runs, and the boy follows. The couple wait, watching for their daughter and the boy to be out of earshot before speaking.

"Do you think he'll do it?" Rory asks his wife.

"We'll find out soon enough," Joanne answers.

•

A Ferris wheel, the tilt-a-whirl, and a carousel later, Heather feeds a handful of cotton candy to Andy. The confectionery cloud of blue sugar dissolves on his tongue and releases dopamine into his body. He's in bliss.

Damn, how did this happen? I swear I died, and this is heaven! Andy thinks, trying to fully grasp the events of the day. One moment he's inches away from getting face fucked by a serial killer, and the next he's on a dream date with a beautiful girl.

"All of this reminds me of the Saint Patrick's Day

parade," Andy says.

"Saint Patrick?" Heather's tone changes, "the murdering Christian monk? We celebrate St. Patrick's Day for the same reason we drink at a funeral."

"Is that so?" Andy asks.

"It is. Oh, look!" Heather points to a large wooden shaft sticking out of the middle of the field. Andy sees people dancing around it, "the Maypole! Let's go watch. He's about to start."

"Whose starting what?"

"The bard, he's going to tell some Bealtaine stories, it's neat. I know all the stories the bards tell, but it's how they tell them that makes them so cool. And this is Phillip, the best of them, they call him the Dark Son, his stories are scary. Come on, we don't want to miss a word!" she leads him by the hand to an open patch of ground near the performers.

Phillip is a dark-skinned man with a head full of curly black hair, a long mustache, and flowing beard. His dress is similar to Andy's. Blue jeans, a T-shirt and sneakers. But, like many of the attendees, he wears a wreath of yellow flowers around his neck.

"What's up with the yellow flowers?" Andy finally asks Heather.

"The rowan? It's Mountain Ash flowers. It's a tradition started back in Ireland and Scotland, I'm told-" she stops mid-sentence and grips Andy's hand, "shh! He's starting!"

The bard placed a small wood crate at the base of the Maypole and jumped on it. Without amplification, Andy could hear him clear as day from their spot, and in moments found himself enthralled by a tale of gods and curses ...

4

*B*efore the Celts and Gaels aligned
And came to Eire to roam,
The Picts, in painted woad designed
Called Muicinis their home.

Upon the breath of whispered nods
The while the land was tilled,
A time unheard of, men and gods,
Unearthed a void they filled."

Phillip stands on the soapbox, gesturing to his audience, conducting the onlookers as a maestro would an orchestra. A giant red headed man with a thick beard, dressed in a green and blue kilt, stands in front of the bard. Blue spirals encircle his arms. By his side is a raven-haired beauty, carrying a shield and a gigantic claymore sword.

"The greatest warrior there known
Was King Cu Mac Cullhain,
Who sat atop his mighty throne
And leveled foes in pain.

His queen, the maiden of the shield,
This Eimear who he chose
Beside him stood, the battlefield
Was theirs, and so they rose."

More players come out of the crowd to join in, two young girls, one blonde, one brunette, and a curly haired red headed teenage boy. The woman hands the tall man the sword and takes the children in her arms.

"As Inis Fail upheld his might,
His name grew ever strong.
The children born him shared their light,
They buoyed him with song.

Conchobhar, son and heir to all,
His daughters born as well-
Both Eirinn and Rowan stood tall
Among where they would dwell."

An old man with a long, white beard and tall walking staff steps out. He beckons to the Queen and her brood to join him. They do.

"The Grand Arch Druid lent a hand,
His name a well-known thing-
This Myrddin guiding through their land
This great and mighty king.

And for a time, a peace ensued-
The Emerald Isle safe.
But then the Formorian brood
Arrived to cleave and chafe."

A man painted in red and white comes into view. He runs around to the onlookers, menacing them, pinching flowers off their necklaces and headdresses.

"With Balor One-Eye as their chief,
Barbarians arrived
Destroying all with no relief
In dragon ships they prized.

They raided up and down the coast,
A trail of lust and greed.
Destruction was their craven host;
They raped and made men bleed."

"The soldiers from the king arrived
But never could engage.

The raiders pillaged and they thrived
Upon their sense of rage.

A bolder notion took control
And Mac Cullhain grew hot.
His cattle stolen as the goal
Enraged him on the spot."

The curly red-haired teen joins the tall man, and the two chase the painted demon around the Maypole until the father and son actors fall down from being dizzy. The demon runs off and hides in the crowd.

A woman in a black gown comes out and helps the tall man to his feet.

"Now in his hubris, off he went
To gather back his herd,
But up above and on his scent,
A darkened scheming bird-

The Mórrigan, the Banshee Queen,
Invoked Goddess of War-
Invited herself to the scene
Intent to claim her score."

The woman in black attempts to hold the tall man. He turns his head and pushes her away.

As Mac Cullhain prepared for bed,
The Phantom Queen appeared.
She uttered something in his head,
But nothing in him feared.

However, there was consequence
For each event of pride.
The Mórrigan broke eloquence
For any who denied.

She offered him a chance to bend
And lay with her desire,
Prepared to steal from Balor wind
And share with Mac her fire.

Blinded by rage, the woman in black prances
about, cursing the man.

"Be gone from me, you temper beast!
I need no help but mine.
In Inis Fail, I dwell and feast;
For all my kin, I shine!

I cast you out and move ahead-
I will not touch your skin.
Be rid from me, I will not bed
Nor dare to let you in!"

His loyalty to home and wife;

To children of his loin
Expelled from him his normal life;
A curse was sent to coin:

Ríastrad cú dílis duit
Riamh dílis don lámh a bheathaíonn,
Mac na talún beidh cuma ye 'sa tsúil,
Riamh madraí macánta, buile nach bréag.

"How dare you to deny the gift
My powers could provide!
The words I spoke will forge a rift
And tear you up inside!"

As soon as this trailed swiftly by,
A surge of pain was felt.
The Mórrígan began to fly
As ravens where he knelt.

The woman in black raises her arms, revealing a web of black fabric. She runs away, weaving through the spectators, howling as she goes.

Inside his tent, he writhed and shook
With spasms filled with rage,
And Mac Cullhain embraced the rook
Who brought him to this stage.

He tore his clothes and sought the night

As she tore through the clouds.
A crimson star that caught his sight
Embraced him in her shrouds.

He would not spurn a second time;
The curse completing lust
And as he fell for the sublime,
His body broke, robust.

The tall man falls to the ground writhing in pain. He covers his face under his robes.

The Mórrígan had done her work,
For there within the dark,
The king began to twist and jerk
Ensnared within her mark.

His tendons snapped; the sinews bent;
His bones began to prowl,
And when his canine nose caught scent,
He gave a bellowed howl.

The namesake of the wolf emerged
As he called to his queen.
His primal instincts once submerged
Exploded on the scene.

He stands now, wearing a bronzed wolf's mask with a long, fanged snout. The surface of the mask is decorated in sigils, knots, and triskelion spirals. The red headed teen stands and brandishes the giant claymore.

Conchobhar, his fervent son,
Drew Cucholg to fight-
His father's sword, the only one
To match their ruler's might-

Attacking with all he possessed.
The monster he beheld
Evaded swings and then addressed
The hunger as it swelled.

The man knocks the sword away from the red headed boy and pushes him to the ground. He places a foot on the boy, raising his hands in victory. Then the masked man falls upon the boy.

The wolf leapt up and had a feast;
He tore and ate the boy.
So full, then belly of the beast
Called sleep to its employ.

The red headed teen throws a handful of something into the air. A rain of crimson confetti falls all around him.

But when he woke again a man
With soldiers looking on,
He wept for loss within the span
Of darkness until dawn.

His wailing spread o'er Inis Fail;
The loss of Conchobhar.
The more Cullhain began to wail,
To more news traveled far.

The tall man weeps. The tears turn to anger, his queen and daughters join him.

To spite the Mórrigan for this,
He rallied all the men.
The balefires blazed in angered hiss
And he let war begin.

He and his men chased day and night
Until alt last his way
Became the anthem for the fight,
And Balor came to pay.

The family hunts through the crowd until they find the painted demon. The family, now all wearing wolf masks, attack the demon, beating the actor down with their bare hands.

With One-Eye and his raiders done,
His son had been avenged.
They paid with steel and flesh and bone
The while their bodies singed.

And in this day in summer's flame.
The balefires lit remind
That Mac Cullhain had worn his name
In honor he would find.

The raiders gone, the people shaped
The sacrifices sought
And none forgot how love was draped
Or what their king had caught.

Never forget …

ST ROOSTER BOOKS

5

Phillip the bard bows to the crowd, jumps off his box, and is ushered away by young girls in blue linen dresses and yellow flowered torcs. The onlookers give a rousing round of applause.

"The king ate his son? That's fucked up. What happened after that? Did he change into a wolf under the full moon and eat people with pentagrams on their palms? How does the Gypsy poem go? A man who is pure of heart will become a wolf when the moon is full and all that?"

"Oh my, ya said Gypsies!" Heather snorts and laughs at the analogy to the classic Universal horror film. "No, no. No Gypsies. Actually, yer gonna get to hear the rest of the story later tonight."

"Oh yeah? How so?"

"Ma and Pa got company coming over to the house tonight. And one of them will be Phillip, I'm sure he can be coerced into telling us more about King Mac Cullhain. Speaking of which, it's getting late, we're going to need to get back to the truck."

"Good idea, after we talk to Phillip, I'm going to need to get some more sleep before getting back on the road tomorrow. I can't cross the state if I stay here. Wherever here is."

"Yer in Tinker's Falls, New York, in southern Onondaga county. And ya don't have to leave, do ya?"

"That was the plan, I'm grateful and all for everything you've done for me, really, I am. All of this, it's been great. I've had a good time and you made me forget about that asshole. Thanks. Maybe I can stop back when I pass through on my way home in fall."

"Fall? What about now? Have ya forgotten about me?" the anger over his inappropriate joke disappears from her face.

"No, I mean, you're standing in front of me right now, how could I forget you?" Andy sees the girl close her eyes and purse her lips for a kiss, "oh no, Heather, I shouldn't do that," he says and steps back from her. *The crazy won't end,* Andy says to himself, *everyone wants to fuck me today!*

"Talk about life imitating art," she says, shaking her head in bewilderment, "what do ya mean? It's only a kiss."

"Yeah, but I just met you this afternoon, plus the way you've been acting, I don't think that's a good idea. Not to mention your parents are here and they did tell us to behave."

"They were being silly. Now yer being sillier. Kiss me."

"Maybe later, okay?" Heather's persistence bothers Andy, he's relieved when her parents join them.

"The god provides," she says in response.

"Are we ready?" Mr. Brannigan asks the teenagers, "the McEntires will be at the house soon for the Bealtaine blessing."

"The McEntires?" Andy asks.

"Old family friends of ours," Mrs. Brannigan answers, "it feels like we've known them for a hundred years."

•

When they near the Brannigan farm, Andy can see bonfires lighting up the property surrounding the Brannigan farm. A dozen cars and trucks are parked in the muck near the property. A throng of people, including Phillip, mill about near the barn. Mr. Brannigan parks the truck nearby.

How many McEntires are there? Andy wonders,

noting at least a dozen faces watching them arrive. Some he recognizes from the Field Days. All of the females are wearing blue sundresses of some design. *What is this? A blue sundress contest?*

An attractive woman breaks away from the group. Tall, with big, blonde hair held back by a barrette laced with yellow flowers, she approaches the Brannigans. A smile fills her face.

"Heather darling," she says.

"Hello, Erin!" Heather shouts with glee, "it's been too long!" the women embrace.

"Far too long, chick."

"Did Rose come?"

"Yes, she's on a break from school. She's over talking to your mom. So, is this the stray hunk you found in your backyard?" Erin looks Andy up and down as Heather confirms her friend's assumptions.

"Yeah, we did a background check on him. He's alright. No priors, right sexy?" Heather says to Andy.

"Yeah, no priors. Pleased to meet you-"

"Erin McEntire," she offers a hand to shake. Andy takes it, her grip is firm and strong. She squeezes his hand before releasing, bringing a small wince from the teenager, "my family owns the neighboring apple orchard, Mac Tire Farms."

"That's cool! I bet you like apples," Andy regrets making the quip after he says it. The girls both giggle and shake their heads.

"An apple a day keeps the witch doctor away," the girls say in chorus, then Erin adds, "so, they're getting ready for the circle and the dedication, we should go over to the mound."

"The mound?" Andy asks.

"Uath Mound, it's where we found ya. The well in the backyard, it's atop the mound."

"What is this, some religious cult thing and you're trying to induct me? The god provides and all that?" The girls' pick their laughter back up in earnest at this comment.

"No, silly. Well, maybe? The god does provide, right Erin?" Heather shrugs her shoulders.

"Yep. The god provides. He really is cute, and funny," Erin says then sighs aloud. Heather nods before explaining it to him.

"It's an old country tradition. The well is a representation of life and prosperity. We'll form a circle around the well, and the elders will tell some stories. It's like an Elk's lodge, only they don't wear funny hats. My mother is the Bandrui, the leader of the bunch, and Erin's father, Jack, is the Cathain, he's like a bailiff at a court. They'll do their annual ritual, and then we," she winks at Andy, "I mean you, can go to bed."

"Oh, really. So, I get to hear the rest of the story now?" Andy asks.

"Yep," Heather continues her reply with a

surprise attack kiss, catching him on the lips, "I knew I could getcha once," the girl wiggles her eyebrows, grabs his hand, and leads him away to the mound.

She takes Andy to stand near her mother and father at the top of the small hill. Erin joins her mother, father, and a raven-haired sister. She whispers something to the brunette, then points at him. He can hear the girl's laughter.

Just what I needed. All the women are laughing at me tonight, he thinks and shakes his head.

"Thank you for coming, friends, neighbors, kinfolk," Mrs. Brannigan says. The guests cease their small talk and give her all of their attention, "I welcome thee to Uath Mound, and the well of the god. Tonight, we gather to pay thanks for the sacrifices made by our ancestors. The god provides. Sláinte."

"Sláinte!" everyone but Andy says in response.

"And now," Mrs. Brannigan continues, "I present to you the bard of Uath Mound Grove, our darkest son, fresh off an award-winning oration at the Field Days, Phillip Dorchester," the circle of attendees applauds and the bard steps forward, bowing as he does.

"This is the part you were waiting for," Heather whispers to Andy. She squeezes his hand tight in anticipation.

"I guess so. I hope it's as good and fucked up as

the first part was," he whispers back.

"You better believe it is," she blows Andy a kiss, and turns her attention to the bard.

6

The bard sets his soapbox at the foot of the well, on the top of the mound. He steps on top of it and begins his grandiose presentation anew. Phillip tells the story in the same manner as before, only now, the actors have changed. The senior McEntire took the role of the cursed king, stepping away from his wife and daughters to stand by the well. Strapped to his back is a sheathed claymore.

To live with this- the curse he bore
Was more than he could stand.
His burdens weighed him all the more;
He feared his changing hand.

His wife and daughters could be next-

And so he came to seek
The wisdom Myrddin hid in text.
The Druid came to speak:

Mrs. Brannigan walks forward, holding a gnarled and withered wooden staff. She stands before Mr. McEntire and shakes her head.

"The curse of gods are far beyond
What mortal men can do.
In truth you must undo the bond
In order to free you.

In doing so, your wife will live;
Your daughters just the same.
A blessing now a god must give
To free your tainted name."

But Mac Cullhain looked on confused.
"Where must my two feet trod?"
And Myrddin looked ok quite amused-
"Why, so another god!

The secret there can breach the curse,
But know the price is high.
I gather things could be much worse.
Your family all could die.

So go and find who dwells inside,

And then you will be free.
I send you forth in eager stride,
No go! Be gone from me."

Mr. McEntire draws out his massive claymore, sticks the blade into the earth at the base of the well and kneels before it. Phillip lights a lantern and holds it aloft with an outstretched hand. The lantern's light casts a shadow falling off Mrs. Brannigan, who is standing with her head bent forward. Her shadow gives the illusion of a crooked, appendage sticking out of the well. The shadow puppet hovers in the air before Mr. McEntire. A hush comes across the attendees.

The words befell on swiftest feet,
And Mac Cullhain went forth.
He searched for one who would complete
His journey heading north.

He came to Crom Cruach at last,
The one who forged his sword-
The Wolf Cleaver, the blade and blast,
And offered him a word.

"I seek your aid, oh god of old!"
An echo pressed before
The open well of stories told.
"And here I am for more.

What can old Crom Cruach surmise
To help one such as you?
A faithful man to wife and skies;
A soldier through and through.

The God of Plenty finds your worth
The sort that I will aid."
His speech propelled a since of mirth;
Upon the air it stayed.

"I want the curse upon me gone.
The riastrad removed."
The god laughed loudly in his tone-
"My lad it has been proved-

This is no curse, a gift indeed!
A blessed to behold."
The king said, "I have made men bleed!
The son I cannot hold.

Devoured and lost, so tell me why?
How can this be for good?"
The god gave a soft reply,
"Let this be understood-

Mr. Brannigan grabs Andy by an arm. Another one of the attendees, a younger man with a thin goatee and long hair tied back in a ponytail, takes his other arm.

"Hey man, what the fuck are doing? Let me go. Heather, what's going on?" Andy demands, resisting the men. They hold him still for Heather.

"Just go with them, don't fight it," she says.

"Don't fight what? What are they-" she puts a finger on his lips and presses it in. Andy stops talking. The smell of mint tickles his nose. He tastes it around his lips. It numbs his tongue. He wants to speak but his mouth won't cooperate.

The numbing spreads through his person.

The riastrad has given all,
And now your family, too,
Can answer to the full moon call;
All wolfing beside you!

No other will be eaten, lad.
Now go, take leave and trust."
And Mac Cullhain left feeling glad
With this truth to adjust.

And he would come back to the well
When balefires burned again
To seek the blessing of the spell;
The one of wolf and man.
Never forget ...

"Remember the great king of Inis Fáil, Cú Mac

Cullhain. On the day we light the Bale Fires and cast out the invaders, when we take heed of the sacrifices made by our ancestors to the gods of old.

The god provides. Never Forget..."

Phillip finishes his presentation, steps off his soapbox, and moves away from the well, joining the rest.

Andy doesn't feel the need to fight Mr. Brannigan and his friend anymore and lets them drag him over to the tallest standing stone. A pair of silent men are waiting for them with ropes. They tie Andy to the stone. He can't feel a thing, his body is numb.

But he can hear.

A ticking echo fills the mound, amplified by the well. He heard this before. Earlier in the day, when the Bad Man whipped his cock out. Right before Andy's luck took a turn for the weirder.

And he can see.

He wishes he couldn't.

7

Unable to do anything but observe, Andy watches the chittering nightmare rise from the well. The ambient light of balefires reflects off brackish water dripping from a segmented, armored exoskeleton. Thin limbs tipped in pincers, bent like leafless branches, grasp the frame of the well's pitched canopy. A roar fills the grove, shaking the wood and stone of the structure.

The thing's massive, chimeric head thrusts forward from under the canopy. Part serpentine and part insectoid and covered in armored scales, a single, red eye turns within its orbital socket. It stares through the souls of all present until focusing on Andy Rivers, tied to a standing stone.

A single, fiery red eye is set into the top of the thing's cranium, above the mouth. Six pairs of vicious mandibles open, exposing a circular maw lined with tusks and filled with a triskelion of spiraling, pointed teeth. The rim of a pair of glasses hangs off the joint of one of the thing's tusks. This doesn't escape Andy's attention.

The Bad Man's glasses? Andy wonders, *this thing ate the Bad Man?*

The creature roars a second time.

It saved me? And now it's going to eat me, too?

"Siobhán Bandrui, Myrddyn of Uath Mound, stands before your all-seeing eye, great Crom Cruach!" Mrs. Brannigan declares and raises her arms with the staff held in her hands. Mr. McEntire stands, drawing his massive claymore from the ground, "the faithful come to bask in your eternal glory. The god provides. Sláinte."

"Sláinte!" the congregation replies. The creature's head sways to and fro. A low, steady chittering rumbles from within its carapace.

Mr. McEntire moves next to Mrs. Brannigan and pulls a familiar wolf mask over his face.

Holy shit. It's the same prop from the Field Days, Andy realizes. Fear begins to set in as he understands why they've tied him to the stone. *They really do mean to feed me to this fucking thing.*

Heather steps up with a small scythe-like knife and cuts Andy's AC/DC t-shirt off, exposing his bare chest.

"Sorry about that. But it was already ripped," the girl says to him. He watches McEntire tap the sword blade on the creature's back, prompting it to move toward Andy. Helpless, he can only watch the thing inch closer to him. It dances about, sniffing the teenager with thin antennae.

"Who so claims this son of the land?" Mrs. Brannigan asks those present.

"I do, Myrddyn," Heather steps forward and curtsies to her mother. Andy watches the bizarre scene unfold, awaiting the moment they will send their giant bug god in for the kill.

"Who be thee?"

"I be Ærika Brighty Branagáin, heir to the Draoícht and next Bandrui Keeper of Uath Mound."

"Do ye vouch for his purity of heart?"

"Aye," she nods, "I vouch for his purity."

"So, mote it be," Mrs. Brannigan says, "today we keep our promise to the god of the land. We light the bale fires and bring unto him a new son to replace he who was lost in yore. The god provides. Sláinte," the congregation repeats her closing word as she points to Andy, and motions to Mr. McEntire. The man double taps his sword on the creature's back. It lunges at Andy one last time.

He watches the monster's mouth open before closing his eyes. It strikes him in the chest. Andy can feel it bite into his breast. Then, instead of devouring him, it releases, and pulls back.

A trail of mucus and blood connects Andy to the creature before it drips to the ground. He can see the wound it left behind, an imprint of the thing's triskelia maw.

Prompted by McEntire and his sword, the thing rears back to the well, and retreats. The chittering of its feet echo as the god slinks down the shaft of its lair.

"Have ye settled on a name for your chosen, Ærika Brighty Branagáin?"

"Aye, that I have, Myrddyn," Heather winks at Andy as she acknowledges her mother's role as Bandrui of Uath Mound. He's still helpless, unable to protest, "A warrior he be, thus a warrior he shall remain. I dub thee Áindle Branagáin."

"A strong name, indeed. So mote it be. The god provides. Sláinte," the gathered folk repeat her blessing.

"That should do ya, love" Heather says and slaps a handful of grasses and mud on the wound, sealing it, "I knew ya were pure of heart," she adds then hugs him.

A light applause grows from the witnesses in attendance. Mr. McEntire sheaths his claymore and pulls the wolf mask off his head. He approaches Mr. Brannigan.

"He'll make a fine son-in-law, Rory," he says, and pats his friend on the shoulder.

Son-in-law? Andy would say if he could speak.

"I remember when Joanne found me," Mr. Brannigan says, "back then I had a different name, too. I don't even remember it now. I swear it was a hundred years ago. I just came home from the war, a hero with nowhere to go. She gave me the same tests on Bealtaine. I passed them, too."

"Oh, I know, I was there, remember? It seems like it was a hundred years ago," Mr. McEntire says.

"It sure does, Jack" Mr. Brannigan and Mr. McEntire untie the ropes binding Andy to the stone. The drugged teenager slips down the face of the standing stone. Heather pulls him up to his feet. Andy feels the numbness leaving his flesh and bones. The poultice covering his wound falls off, revealing a blue stained tri-spiral pattern.

"Welcome to the family," Heather tells Andy. She holds him close, touches her lips to his, and kisses him. Andy doesn't fight her; he accepts the passionate embrace. For the first time in sometime, Andrew Rivers-*No Áindle Brannigan*, he reminds himself-doesn't feel the urge to move on. No, now he feels right at home.

The god provides.

4 LAMMAS

A WITCHING DOWN THE HOLLER

ST ROOSTER BOOKS

A WITCHING DOWN THE HOLLER

Beholden to the eye of the Sun,
Lugh looked down upon all creations,
And blessed them with everlasting life.
Of Man, and raven, and of wolf.

Drúi holy text fragment,
Converted from the original Pict ogham.

ST ROOSTER BOOKS

1

The wind cries and brings terror with it. Storm clouds and lightning carry the banshee wail, rolling on thunder past the crescent of the moon. The breath of summer blows from the south and west. It cascades across the rolling foothills, growing in power and intensity as it flows over the land.

The gusts assault the homesteads and farms settled throughout the region. They strike through the fields, picking up speed, racing across the flatlands in the valley. Dairy cattle shiver in panic within their stalls while the residents of the Foothills hide inside their beds. The howling gusts speak for their fear, invading their dreams, providing affirmation of the terrors of the night.

Abandon all hope, the voice of despair says to

the inhabitants.

Shutters, doors, and shingles rattle in fearful response. The winds seep through the walls of the buildings, spreading paralyzing terror throughout those sleeping within. Outside, the hills and shifting clouds ensure no stars or sources of light can be seen.

Except for a solitary twinkle in the night.

A patch of sunflowers, their heads bent in prayer, fight the wind and stand watch over a small clearing in an orchard, near a stretch of corn fields. From within, a flickering light shines in the darkness. Inside walls of sunflower stalks, alone in her sanctuary, a woman fucks with ancient, cyclopean things she shouldn't.

She does it for love and blood.

The girl sits within a pentagram, drawn in chalk. Arcane symbols are scrawled around the circle, and candles burn at each point of the star. A wolf's skull, adorned with the horns of a bull, decorates the center of the star. A sixth candle, melting down the curve of the cranium, stands out from a hole in the bone.

Desire radiates in her eyes, reddened and pink from the madness of compulsion. Sweat clings to her exposed flesh, gluing strands of black hair to her face. She pants with lust, moaning and squeaking with each breath. Her heart, pounding through her chest, can be heard over the winds. It keeps time when time no longer matters.

She holds the skull in her hands. Ancient and unholy to some, the relic has grown a coppery patina lacquer during its thousand-year slumber. Words not heard by men in eons flow from the woman's lips.

An Badhbh- Bronntanas na beatha
An Badhbh- An Scriosóir
An t-anam Badhbh-Éillithe
An Badhbh- Cuirim fáilte romhat abhaile

They call out to the beyond, summoning powers long lost from this realm.

The power she seeks answers.

Outside of her circle, the wind focuses on the land, striking it with a hurricane's force. A taste of the love she seeks cascades through her. An orgasm floods her body with hormones, exacerbating the visions of her love and desire. She kneels in submission, enveloped in the moment.

Around her, the candles blow out in succession of the elements: Earth, Fire, Water, Air, and Spirit. The glowing candle in the skull holds back the void of darkness. It casts a crimson shadow across her grinning face, masking the woman in a visage of madness. She sits motionless, transfixed in the moment.

A clamor breaks her from the catatonic trance.

Something rustles the sunflowers, vibrating and shaking them. Dust rises up in the clatter, floating in the air about her. The girl falls to her side laughing in glee, holding the skull aloft with one hand. She bites at her free hand, stopping to savor the blood seeping from the wounds.

It all stops.

She sucks on her fingers. Pink saliva drips into the dirt. Silence settles in, broken only by the blowing winds. A light tapping of flower stalks continues the clatter. It grows in volume and speed until there is an explosion of sunflowers and leaves.

A gigantic crow hops through, holding something in its long beak. Thick, black fur covers one side of the infernal package. From the other, viscous, congealed ichor drips onto the floor. A large predatory animal, a canine, now missed its skin.

If it still lived.

The bird spreads its wings, and with a single flap, flies across the clearing, and lands at the edge of the magical circle. The girl rolls over, kneeling before the large, jet black avian. She holds the skull in her hands forward as an offering, hyperventilating. The bird opens its beak and drops the gory cargo to the floor. The raw animal pelt lands with a wet plop.

The power she has sought sits inches away from her fingertips. She will soon possess it, she puts all doubt aside. But it comes with a steep price, albeit one she prepared herself to pay when she resolved to follow through with this ritual. Yet even with preparation, seeing this come to fruition becomes as surreal as the magic used to summon it.

The enormous bird shrieks, breaking her frozen state. It spreads its wings, revealing the truth of its being to the girl. A vision of all-consuming cosmic insanity strikes her dumb with fright. She cries in exalted terror, but no sound comes forward. The feathered limbs grow and engulf the room, extinguishing the crimson haze of the skull.

From behind this curtain of darkness, she accepts the gifts bestowed upon her. The woman's mind howls in ecstatic agony, paying for her carnal lust with the last of her humanity.

She howls aloud, singing to her love.

An Mac Tíre mo ghrá...

The Wolf, my love.

The woman embraces her damnation.

2

The sun smiles on the foothills. The giant eye looks down upon the earth, gracing all under its glow. It gives life, and takes life, in a constant cycle. Within a home next to an apple orchard, a cloud of flour captures the sunlight filtering through a window.

The rays shine on the dining room table where Peggy Mac Tire and her young daughters, little Rosie and Erin, are making bread. Smiles fill their pre-teen faces. A frantic banging on the door startles Peggy and the girls, distracting them from their task.

"Stay put, the both of ya," she tells the girls, and sets her rolling pin aside. Erin, the older of the two girls by a year, snatches up the wooden cylinder. Peggy wipes her hands off in her apron before pulling it off and draping it across the caning of a chair.

The mystery solicitor continues to pound on the door, rattling the frame, until Peggy opens it. Standing on the porch she sees a woman, shaking with rage. Matted tresses stick to her face, her dress is stained and filthy. An awful odor comes off her person.

"Ye finally open the door, Goody Mac Tíre," her words are laced with venom and contempt. Peggy is far too familiar with the wretch.

She's an owl in an ivy bush, Peggy keeps the insult to herself. She knows better than to antagonize the woman.

Emmy O'Sullivan lived down in the hollow for as long as they could remember, and the Mac Tíre's had long memories, indeed. Some call the reclusive woman a witch. To Peggy Mac Tíre, she's a pain in the ass. But the Mac Tíre matron, ever a magnanimous and proper lady, doesn't allow this to reflect in her demeanor. She remains polite.

"Hello, Emmy. How can I help you?"

"Where is he? I heard talk he came back home from the war."

"That he did. His family missed him while he was gone."

"I should be his family. He was my man before

ye came around. Always was me man. Ye stole him from me, harlot!" Emmy spits the words out. Peggy shakes her head, a look of disappointment on her face.

"I can't help that he chose me over ye. I will say this. Ya threw yerself at him, and he told ya to feck off, did he not? It is what it is. Now if that will be all-"

"It shan't be all. Ye bewitched him, to get his blood, 'tis what ye did! Ye be *fae*, I know it to be so," Emmy's accusation humors Peggy. But instead of laughing at the woman, she keeps a calm tone.

"*Fae*? Superstitious fairy tales, again, Emmy? Why would I want his blood? Are ya daft?"

"His blood is pure, it's the blood of Kings."

"What are ya doing, Emmy? Dipping into the cider, rambling about nonsense, and being disguised at this time of the day?"

"I ain't been sippin' on no spirits! Ye be a changeling!"

"I'm no changeling, Emmy O'Sullivan," Peggy almost loses her temper, "It doesn't matter. Yer not welcome here, Emmy," Peggy tells her, still maintaining her composure. *The woman some believe is a witch,* she thought, *is accusing me of bewitching. How this defines irony!*

"A pox on ye, Goody Mac Tire, and thy spawn!" is her reply.

And now she's throwing curses around!

"Bite yer tongue, woman!" Peggy shoots back, "I'll not have ya casting words at me. How dare ya."

"I do as I like, y'all will see."

"I don't want to be rude to ya, Emmy. Please, let it be, and leave the children out of it if ya can't. Don't ya be dragging them into this, they're innocents."

"Unlike their father and mum," Emmy curls her lip in disgust and spits on the floor at Peggy's feet, "where's he at? He's not here, is he? Otherwise, he woulda answered the door."

"That's not for ya to worry about. Now, please, move along. Don't make me ask ya a third time to take yer leave. Good day, Emmy, I'm sorry it's come to this," Peggy closes the door on Emmy, and waits until she hears their guest walk down the steps and leave. She listens, to make sure Emmy left, then returns to the table with her daughters, where they resume making bread.

"Who was that, mummy?" Rosie asks her mother, breaking the silence.

"I saw her," Erin adds, "she looked like the Digger Do. I had the rolling pin ready," she jabs her smaller sister in the ribs with an elbow.

"Be nice to me or the Digger Do'll getcha," Rosie pushes her sister back.

"Oh, don't be silly girls. It was just Emmy talking crazy again. Ya promise me y'all stay away from her and her cottage," Rosie and Erin shook their heads in unison, "good, now we won't talk about no Digger Do around yer daddy or brother, they don't need to know, daddy'll only get upset. Let's get to baking this bread. The men'll be home after sunset and they'll be famished from working all day."

·

The setting sun colors the sky red, and shadows fall across the homesteads in the valley. A translucent crescent moon rises to meet Mars and Venus, each a celestial signpost of the night to come. A murder of crows circles the fields, riding the warm summer air currents. They see everything, black eyed observers some say are vessels of Babdh, the Mórrígan, herself.

Underneath the twilight canopy, the Branagáin clan's dairy and farmlands neighbor the Mac Tíre clan's orchards. The proximity allows Jack and Conner Mac Tíre the luxury of walking home through the cornfields. Magnificent in midsummer, the stalks of corn, grown to feed the Branagáin's Devon milking cows, are tall and lush. The golden tips, bent from the previous night's summer storm, gaze down upon the father and son, watching them pass.

"You did good work today, Conner. I'm proud of ya, lad." Jack says to his son, "Mr. Branagáin was pleased with the way the barn is coming along. At this rate the work'll be done for fall. It'll make a fine home for their milking cattle when the snow falls."

"Thank you, daddy," the boy replies. A straw hat covers his red hair and overalls cover his lank frame.

"You're welcome, lad."

"Daddy, can I ask you something?" Conner Mac Tire's face reflects a deep, lingering concern for something.

"What is it? Don't you ever feel like you can't ask me something, unless it's inappropriate men talk around the women folk," Jack assures his son.

"How bad was it? The war, I mean?"

"War is bad and good, lad," Jack Mac Tire replies to the teenage boy. *He's almost a man, like me, before all this warring,* the family patron keeps to himself.

"Were ya afraid, daddy?"

"Of course, I was afraid. It's natural to be terrified when you're facing death, and hearing the banshees calling the men standing beside you. I pissed my pants more than once, which is better than I can say for most men. But I survived, and it's over."

"They say yer the bravest. That yer the Cathain."

"Aye, lad. Now I'm the Cathain," the honor of Cathain, bestowed upon the bravest of the clan at Uath Mound, often fell upon war veterans such as

Jack. He accepted the role with pride.

"Did you see her?"

"See who?"

"You know, her," the teen points to the crows flying in the sky. Jack shakes his head.

"Am I standing here right now, talking to ya, lad?"

"Aye."

"Then ya have your answer."

"I'm glad the war is over, and you are home."

"Me, too, lad. Me, too," Jack Mac Tíre pats his teenage son on the back, "I bet your mum and sisters have a nice hot meal waiting for us at home."

"I think I might be too exhausted to eat," Conner admits.

"Now don't be telling your mum that, especially after all the time she-" Jack *feels* it first, a rumbling from the ground. He puts a hand on his son's chest and stops walking.

"What is it Daddy?"

Jack kneels and lays his ear to the ground. He *hears* it. Now his suspicions are confirmed. As he stands the rumble becomes audible.

The rumbling grows in volume, and the shaking earth vibrates their legs until the lowing of dairy cattle can be heard. It's a baleful chorus drifting through the percussion of the ungulates' pounding hooves. Jack grabs Conner and holds the teenager tight to his body.

"It's a stampede, boy. Don't move!" Jack screams at his son, his voice barely audible over the clamor.

A brown and white cow hustles by them, then another, and another. A nonstop, frantic barrage of running dairy cattle. It's the entire Branagáin herd, on the run.

But running from what? Jack wonders as they streak by him and his son until fifty head of dairy cattle have gone by. Jack releases his son. He steps away and adjusts his straw hat. Bits of corn stalks and cow hair fill the air, capturing the remaining sunlight.

"Are you well?" Jack asks his son.

"I think so," Conner replies, then asks his father, "what spooked them?"

A row or two over, corn stalks rustle and snap. He can hear a low, barely audible growl. And both Jack and his son know the answer.

A fecking wolf.

Conner, no more than a yard away, makes eye contact with his father.

"Daddy?" he says. Jack puts a finger up to his lip and shakes his head.

Emerging from the shadows behind them, a large *something* knocks Jack on his ass. His head whips back, stunning the burly man, until a snarling growl brings the elder Mac Tíre back to his senses. He opens his eyes, revealing a scene of terror.

A giant black wolf stands between Jack and Conner. His son is shaking but standing his ground in front of the monster. Jack sees his son's bladder leak, staining the front of the teenager's britches.

"Daddy, I'm not afrai-" Conner doesn't finish his sentence. The wolf lunges, grabbing him by the head with its gigantic maw. The boy's straw hat tumbles to the ground.

"No!" Jack shouts. He jumps to his feet and launches after the black beast. He lands on the thing's backside and grabs ahold, but the animal's powerful hindquarters tear from his grasp. Jack's only reward is a handful of black and gray fur as the monster drags his son away.

The animal scampers and drops its trophy when Conner's foot snags on a cornstalk. This gives Jack the opportunity he needs to recover and mount an offensive. Jack's left fist still clenches a handful of the wolf's black coat. He pulls his tomahawk off his belt with his right hand and throws it at the monster. It tumbles end over end, spinning through the air.

The tomahawk's butt spike sticks into the wolf's face.

The monster squeals in agony and shakes its head until it falls out, pulling the wolf's left eye with it. A squirt of brackish blood spurts out of the wound, covering the plants and ground in a crimson gout. Jack can see the animal's eyeball sticking to the tomahawk's spike. It stares back at him.

The weapon's toe sticks into the earth next to the teenager's prone body, providing the wolf's extracted eyeball a front row seat of the proceedings. Snarling, the animal sinks its teeth into Conner's shoulder and drags him out of Jack's reach. The beast reaches full speed before it disappears into the darkness and rows of corn.

"Conner!" The teen's father screams and falls to his knees, weeping, repeating his son's name over, and over. The beast's eye taunts him, glistening in the waning twilight. A crow swoops down and away, scooping the eyeball up with its beak as it passes by.

Sean 'Jack' Chulainn Mac Tíre's cries echo through the valley and into the night...

3

Dots of light from torches and lanterns flicker in the night, moving throughout the Branagáin farm cornfield. A large search party combs the fields looking for a lost member of their flock. The faithful of Uath Mound call out their quarry's name.

"*Conner!*" echoes from a myriad of voices.

Their search is in vain.

Lanterns illuminate the roofed porch of the Mac Tíre homestead. Sitting together on a rocking swing, Jack holds Peggy Mac Tíre, consoling her. The bruised bags under their eyes betray the tears they've cried. Inside their home, their young daughters have cried themselves to sleep after learning of their brother's abduction. Now, the parents, exhausted from a long day followed by an unexpectedly long night, find themselves falling asleep when their neighbor walks up the steps.

"Anything?" Jack asks his friend.

"We secured all the Devons, thankfully. But

your boy and the wolf? Nay," Flynn Branagáin says as he shakes his head, "lost its trail at the edge of the field, down by the holler. The dogs can't pick it back up either. It disappears, like the bastard flew away."

"I wounded the bastard pretty good; I know I did. It had to bleed to death by now," Jack says, *or my son bled to death,* he keeps to himself. He fears the latter is the truth.

"I don't know, we did find a lot of blood, I won't deny that. But I do know people are tired, it's getting near midnight, so I'm sending them home. We'll get back to it at first light in a few hours. I'm sorry, Jack, Margaret, but you know if a wolf takes someone, the odds of them being found alive are slim," Flynn drops his head.

"Don't be sorry, Flynn, ya didn't take our son," Peggy replies, "please tell everyone thank ya for all they've done."

"I will, Goody Mac Tíre," Flynn bows his head and tips his felt tricorn.

"Goodnight, Flynn," Jack says. Flynn Branagáin nods in reply and leaves. Jack and Peggy wait until he's entered the cornfield before retiring themselves. A long day awaits them on the morrow. Jack Mac Tíre collapses on his bed from exhaustion. Sleep follows.

The war returns with it.

•

nside a fort's outer blockhouse, surrounded by a sea of dead, a candle's flame glows from within a Jack O' Lantern. Flickering shadows paint the faces of the men stationed within. Among them is Jack Mac Tire, garbed in the furs and skins of trappers, and armed for the wilderness. Together, they are Rangers serving in the Continental Army.

Fear grips these men. Huddled together in a circle, they clench their muskets with white knuckles. Long bayonets, attached to the rifle barrels, extend out from the throng of men creating a formidable picket.

It does nothing to protect them from the sounds of the dying coming from the battlefield.

Or the rotten, fetid stench of death...

Something slams into the wall of the fort, shaking the frame of the structure. Dust erupts from the palisade and creates a cloud in the light. The men hold their breath in unison. The wind whistles louder through the weakened structure, and a noticeable breeze swirls about, extinguishing the candle within the carved turnip. The men stand still, shaking in panic.

The cries of the dying cease and silence grasps the small blockade fort. The jittering of metal fills the enclosed area, as the men tremble in horror.

A terrible wrenching sound breaks the moment. The walls shake until the light of the moon pierces the darkness, illuminating the men inside the fort. Their eyes are emblazoned with terror.

They watch as something superhuman rips a log out of the frame.

Jack can see outside. Surrounding the stock house, a low mist hung halfway up the walls. Hovering in the fog were dozens of shadows and glowing, amber eyes. Twisted and deformed, the shadows surrounded the blockhouse. The soldiers aim their rifles through the exposed opening. The phalanx of shades threatens with pincers of darkness, snapping at the air.

Then they break the mist revealing the shadowy demons to be British Regulars in their scarlet coats.

Except each has a snarling, canid head with glowing yellow eyes.

"Fire!" Jack commands and the Rangers squeeze the triggers of their muskets in unison.

As quick as the hammers fall and fire erupts from the barrels, lighting up the night, the black powder cloud obscures everything. Jack, eyes closed, else they sting and burn from the sulfur cloud, goes through the motions of reloading his weapon with ease. He trained for moments such as these. It's the only reason they are able to get off another volley, creating a screen of deadly lead musket balls. The first waves of Redcoats are cut into pieces. The others step back, blending into the mist.

A mournful howl rises from the mist.

And the fallen rise.

"Oh, my god," Jack curses as he watches the regulars, shot moments ago, stand back up. Parts hang limp off, or behind, their bodies. He makes eye contact with the closest one, but finds his focus distracted by the gaping hole in its lupine head. How can it be walking?

Behind them, the candle comes back to life, the fire within the carved and hollowed turnip grows larger and brighter than before. A shadow cast out from the Rangers, covering the cadaverous nightmares as they shambled forward. Jack can't determine if the light is playing tricks with his mind, but the dead things are not only walking toward the fort, they are moving closer together.

Becoming one entity. Teeth gnash and snap, growing into long fangs with each bite. Dozens of appendages grow out of the sides of the thing, a bubbling, shifting mass of flesh, bone, and cartilage. It roars with the presence of a thunderbolt at ground zero.

It lurches forward and rips away the fort's roof, revealing chaos incarnate. A multi-headed, chimeric abomination with a single giant eye stands before them. Blood drips from the thing's yellow pupil.

Balor, Jack's fear whispers to him. The thing

stares down at Jack and the rangers. The soldiers thrust their bayonets at the thing. It grabs one of the men with a twisted appendage. Jack sees the Ranger's face.

It's Conner.

"See? I'm not afraid, Daddy," he says before screeching like a baby rabbit in a trap as the cyclopean entity devours the boy before him.

Conner's screams raise the hair on Jack's neck and he pisses himself. He steps back, out of the puddle, clipping the Jack O'Lantern with the butt of his musket, sending it tumbling onto a small wooden keg.

Jack feels the impact and watches the shadows move with the light. He turns around and sees the black powder pouring from the keg. In a millisecond, dozens of words flow through Jack Mac Tíre's brain, but none of them are settled on by the time the candle ignites the powder.

The fire burns and purifies...

4

The morning sun wakes Jack from the inferno of his nightmares. Peggy Mac Tíre didn't sleep, her own nightmare, an ever-present void in her being only a mother can understand, prevented the act.

Their daughters, clad in their white linen nightshirts, burst into their parents' bedroom. Erin and Rose are frowning and morose, the color drained from their faces.

"Daddy, mum," Erin asks, "Did they find Conner?" Peggy shakes her head.

"No, no they didn't," Jack sighs after he answers his daughter. He sees the color drain from her face and tears well in her eyes. Peggy sees this, too, and pats a portion of the bed. Erin hops on it and holds her mother's hand.

"I guess that explains why people left food on

our porch," Rosie says. She forces the words out, stifling tears of her own.

"Isn't that what they do when somebody dies, mum?" Erin asks.

"Yes," Peggy says, "yes, it is. It's good manners for yer neighbors to do so."

"Why's that?" Rosie asks.

"We won't have much time to make food for ourselves, preparing a funeral and such as must be done," Jack answers.

"A funeral for ..." Rosie can't bring herself to say his name. She bursts into tears, "did Conner die, mum?" Rosie asks.

"Aye, lass, for Conner. They didn't find him last night, girls. You know these rolling hills are a wilderness, fraught with dangers," Jack says and hugs both of his daughters. Tears roll down the cheeks of each family member as they huddle together to lament the loss of their brother and son.

Once the crying is over, Jack and Peggy open the door to discover the girls weren't kidding around. Before the family reaches the door, delicious aromas of cooked food help them remember their lost appetites.

Words of tragedy travel fast through the foothills, and the Mac Tíres' neighbors respond in kind. Anonymous callers came from Tinker's Falls to Cardiff, and each left something on the Mac Tíres' roofed porch.

Fresh picked flowers, fruits, and vegetables, all blooming for the midsummer festival to come, decorate the veranda. Crocks of soup and stew, feathered and dressed chickens, turkeys and pheasants complete the mourning offering of their neighbors.

The Mac Tires accepted all the gifts, bringing them inside. Some people left calling cards, others remained anonymous. The warm crocks teased their hunger-panged bellies. Peggy places the fresh corn chowder from the Branagáins, with a card signed by the family, near the hearth on their dormant wood stove.

The delicious aroma of the chowder finds itself usurped by the crocked stew. Peggy discovers a note tied to the top of the container. She opens it, surprised to find it's from Emmy O'Sullivan.

"Please forgive my past trespasses and accept my condolences. No family should lose a son so young. Emmy O'Sullivan."

Jack watches his wife read the note and sees her demeanor change from hungry to irritated.

"What is it Peg? Is something wrong?"

"This stew. It's from Emmy. Should we?" Peggy asks Jack.

"Should we what?" he responds.

"Should we keep it? I mean do ya trust her?"

"Why shouldn't I? It smells good, I doubt she's going to poison us and leave a note identifying her as the culprit."

"What is it?"

"Looks like a pork stew."

"Okay, it'd be rude to the pig for us to toss it away."

"Truth be told, that's a fact," Jack says before scooping out a healthy portion with a ladle. Potatoes, carrots and parsnips and chunks of pork floated in the crock. He dumps it into a bowl and soaks up some of the soupy juices with a loaf of bread from the night before.

Jack sits down in his chair at the dinner table. His family joins him, leaving Conner's spot at the table bare. Without a word, no prayer or eulogy, together they feast in honor of their fallen brother and son.

Afterwards, the Mac Tíre women clean up and tend to the dishes. Jack retires to the porch to smoke his pipe and gather his thoughts. The day promises to bring more bad news, of this, he's sure. His thoughts return to the cornfield. He can see his son being dragged away by the wounded beast.

Conner! Covered in black blood, the one-eyed predator dragging him away. The creature's eye, hanging off a tomahawk, staring back at the boy's father before a feathered omen of death swoops in and takes it away.

The Mac Tíre patron shakes his head, hoping it will remove the imagery from his mind. It does not. He's still in the process of lighting the tobacco when Flynn Branagáin walks out of the cornfield. Jack draws a few puffs off the pipe in the time it takes his neighbor to traverse the lawn.

"Top o' the morning, Jack," Flynn says, tipping his tricorn hat with a finger. Jack shakes his hand and follows it up with a hug.

"Aye, good to see you, Flynn. But what does this day bring us but tragedy, my friend," Jack puffs his pipe after replying.

"That's why I've come to fetch you. There's something you need to see back at the farm."

"Oh?" Jack's expression turns from remorse to curious, "what is it?"

"I dare not say it out loud," his face grew ashen, "and bring your big sword, the claymore."

"I have my rifle from-" Flynn throws his hand up and interrupts his friend.

"The sword is steel, no? And last I was told; steel is made from iron?"

"'Tis," Mac Tíre agrees, perplexed at his friend's reaction.

"Bring the fecking sword, Jack."

He retreats into his home and acquires the family heirloom. Peggy doesn't ask why her husband brings his sword with him, or where he's headed to. She knows the sword's purpose. After all, its name is Wolf Cleaver.

And a wolf killed their son.

Peggy and the girls finish their chores soon after Jack leaves. The Mac Tíre matron sits at the table and drinks a cup of sun tea while her daughters bond over knitting a blanket together.

Conner ... she laments her oldest child in thought, *if only I'd been there. What? I'm no Éimear the Shield Maiden. I'd be killed by the wolf, too! And these two waifs, they'd be without a mum.*

"Come on girls, we need to be getting over to the Branagáin's with yer daddy," she tells her daughters, as she searches for something in a cloth satchel with her hand. She withdraws a trio of wooden small charms hanging from leather cords. The surface of each charm is painted with a pentacle. Peggy ties one about her neck with the strip of leather.

"What's that star mum?" Rosie asks.

"It's for protection. Now, I know I told ya girls to stay away from Emmy's cottage," Peggy tells Erin and Rosie, "but we need to be returning her crockery back to her. So, we'll be making a stop there on the way. Ya don't be speaking to her, ya hear me?"

"Yes mum," both girls say in unison.

"Good, now come, I want you each to wear these around your necks."

"Why do we need protection? Is it cos Emmy's a

Digger Do?" Erin quips. Her mother giggles.

"Emmy's no Digger Do. It's better to be safe than not, child," she hands her daughters the charms and they tie them around their necks.

"I like it," Rosie says. Peggy smiles.

"Let's hurry along now, I'm sure everyone is waiting for us at the Mound," and they left their home to return the pottery to its owner.

•

The crows fly above, ever circling about as they observe all transpiring below them.

On the ground, Flynn leads Jack through the cornfield in silence.

As they come upon the spot of Conner's abduction, Jack can feel a pit grow in the bottom of his gut. Blood stains on the earth and crushed corn stalks are the only evidence of the previous night's tragedy. He can hear the wolf snarling.

A ghost image of the night before plays out before him.

Conner! No!

He blinks it away as they arrive at the barn. A throng of men stand near the open doors, each of them terrified.

"What do ya see on the floor?" Flynn points to a lock of hair on the floor of the barn. It's black, curly, and long.

"Hair," Jack replies.

"Aye, hair. Do ya know what it was last night?"

"Hair?" Jack lets out a nervous giggle.

"What kind of hair, though?" Flynn pushes the issue, his tone and demeanor remaining cold.

"Hairy hair? Someone lost a lock of hair. It happens all the time. Why are you being such a dilberry?"

"Jack," Flynn's face turns ashen, his words shake, as he makes the revelation, "this is where the dogs got the scent."

"What do you mean?" Jack's demeanor shifted from curiosity to concern, "why would they be getting the scent in your barn?"

"Because last night," Flynn's words shake in fear, "this pile of hair was the fur you pulled off the wolf's coat."

5

The stench of Emmy O'Sullivan's cottage hangs in the air, nauseating Peggy Mac Tíre well before she reaches sight of the property. It reeks with an eye watering stench as wretched as its occupant's mephitis the day before.

"Why does it smell so bad?" Erin asks her mother, wrinkling her nose in disgust.

"Cos she's the Digger Do!" Rosie adds, copying the face her sister makes.

"Girls, have some manners," Peggy scolds her daughters, "if you keep that look on yer face, it'll freeze there."

"Is that what happened to Emmy?" Erin asks and squinches her eyes and cheeks together. Rosie mimics her sister, again. Their mother snorts to prevent an outward burst of laughter. The girls giggle and menace one another, snarling and hissing, with imaginary fangs in their mouths and mock claws on their outstretched fingertips.

"That's not nice. It's not her fault she's homely, though she might want to plant more flowers to help with the stink," this gets a giggle from the girls, "now come along, let's get this over with," Peggy tells her daughters. Erin and Rosie fall in line without another word.

Peggy knocks on the door with a triple rap. It opens before the third resonates. The delicious scent of stew covers the putrid stench from outside. Emmy, her head covered in a shawl and bowed, looks down at Peggy's feet.

"What is it you need Goody Mac Tíre?"

"Good day, Emmy, I've brought back yer pottery. I wanted to thank ya for yer kindness. We did enjoy the stew," Peggy can't see Emmy's face, but Erin and Rosie can.

"All ye did, eh? Filled yer bellies, did it?" The girls can see her smile as she asks.

"Aye, it did. Thank ya."

"No need to be thankin' me, Goody Mac Tíre," the girls watch Emmy's smile grow into a mask of insanity, her dimples stretching out, her teeth, pitted and black, poking from her lips, "'twas me pleasure to help in yer time of loss," Emmy takes the pottery from Peggy with gnarled and twisted hands. The woman stands, her shawl falls across her face, covering the left side of it. "Thank ye for returning these. Ye have a pleasant day now," Emmy says, and closes the door with a foot.

Are you serious? Peggy exhibits willpower in not pushing the issue with Emmy. The less the better. Peggy takes her daughters by the hand and leads them away, toward Uath mound.

When they reach the edge of the cornfield at the Branagáin farm, Rosie tugs on her mother's sleeve.

"Mum?"

"Yes?"

"What happened to Emmy's eye?"

"What do you mean?" She stops in her tracks, her tone turning cold. Rosie, stunned by the sudden change in her mother's demeanor, shuts up. "Well? Speak, child!" Peggy commands her daughter.

"Yesterday when Emmy came to the house, she had two, mum," Peggy could confirm this to be true. Nothing seemed amiss with the woman's eyes the day before, "today, she's missing one."

"Are ya certain of this?" Peggy asks her daughter.

"Yes, mum. I could see it when her head was bowed."

"I saw it, too," Erin volunteers.

"Which eye?" The baying of hounds echoes down through the hollow.

"This one," Rosie and Erin each point to their own left eye as they reply in harmony.

•

Led by a trio of hounds, a half dozen men from Tinker's Falls march down the road. They come from the foothills, Uath Mound, and the Branagáin farm. There's Fergus McSweeney the miller, and Cillian Kelley who raises goats and chickens. Ronan Walsh and his son Donny, the smiths, come with their wolfhounds. Also among them is Flynn Branagáin and Jack Mac Tíre. They are armed with their family swords, sheathed on their backs. The others carry the tools of their trades, ranging from scythes to pitchforks and hammers.

The dogs direct them, dragging their handlers forward. After losing the scent of their quarry the night before, they take up the chase with enthusiastic vigor. Ahead of them, down the road, a woman and two children stand to the side, waiting by the tall rows of corn.

"Say, Jack, ain't that yer load of mischief?" Flynn asks, pointing to the trio.

"It sure is. They would be heading to your farm, I would think," Jack replies out loud, and ponders to himself, *but why this way?* Taking the road added a half mile onto the walk between Spruce Pond and Uath Mound.

The dogs pull the men closer, and within a few

minutes, the hunters reach Peggy and her daughters. The Mac Tíre matron intercepts them. The dogs bark like mad at Peggy, but she ignores them. She wastes no time kissing her husband on the cheek.

"I'm so very happy to see you right now, love," she says. He notices she is trembling.

"Peggy, dear, what's a matter? You're shaking. You and the girls shoulda gone through the field, you'd be at the farm by now," Jack tells her.

"Oh, Jack, I'm terrified right now. Something's afoot with Emmy O'Sullivan," she tells her husband.

"Emmy, you say? Why's that?" Jack twists his beard as she tells him. When she finishes, he kisses her forehead. "Go, get to the farm, Moira is waiting for you and the girls. A wolf hunt ain't no place for them."

"Wolf hunt? How sure are we of that, now?" Flynn interjects, "if what the children say is true, then this becomes another beast all together, Jack."

"I don't want to rush to make accusations of witchcraft and sorcery. I know what I saw, what took my boy away. And a wolf it was, of that I'm certain. It looked me in the eye."

A single amber eye, burning a hole through Jack's skull. And he's back in the cornfield, the evening before, the wolf staring at him, taunting him. Jack throws his tomahawk at the beast.

It strikes. A splash of blood fills his vision, dripping away, revealing a single, amber eye floating in the air.

Staring at him.

Conner!

"Jack, come to yer senses, man, are ya with us?" Flynn waves a hand in front of Jack Mac Tire's face, bringing him back to the now.

"Aye, Flynn!" he replies, shaking his head, "set the dogs loose. I bet they go visit Emmy's cottage."

"Are ya sure of that?" Flynn asks. Jack looks to Peggy, who nods in reply.

"That I am," Jack nods to the handlers, and they release the hounds. Barking and snarling, streams of spit hanging from their lips, the dogs run down the road at top speed. It doesn't take them long to arrive at their destination.

Emmy O'Sullivan's cottage.

"Well, isn't that a hoot?" Jack asks nobody in particular and pulls Wolf Cleaver from its scabbard.

6

The hounds stand on their hind legs, scratching at Emmy's cottage door. They snarl and bite at the air as a never-ending supply of spittle paints the area surrounding the door. The men are close behind their dogs. Jack Mac Tire leads the way at the forefront with his claymore on point.

The handlers whistle a command, telling the hounds to heel. The canines do so with reluctance, continuing to snarl at the ramshackle cottage. Once the animals are secured, Jack steps forward and knocks on the cottage door.

"Open up, Emmy O'Sullivan, I know yer in there," Jack demands as his fist pounds the wood, shaking the frame, "open up or I'll-"

A screeching howl builds in volume from within the cottage. The hounds bolt from their handler's grip, running for their lives back to the farmstead. Mac Tire backs away from the door and holds his sword with two hands, preparing for whatever may come. A murder of crows bursts from the trees. The exodus creates a clamor of fluttering wings and squawking birds.

Silence follows.

"Emmy, what sort of shenanigans do ya have going on here?" Jack breaks the quiet, "we've only come to talk to ya!" he insists.

And to see yer fecking eye, Jack adds to himself.

Flynn pushes Jack to his feet. He steps up and raps on the door, again. On the third knock ...

It opens.

From inside, the delicious aroma of Emmy's stew greets Jack Mac Tíre, covering the exterior's stink. The cottage is full of things, but none of them are Emmy O'Sullivan.

The interior is a cluttered mess, strewn with miscellanea. Dried herbs and the withered husks of dead fauna, hanging by foot or talon, are connected by cobwebs coated in dust. Carved gourds and turnips line shelves. A cauldron rests on the coals of the hearth, simmering the contents.

"Emmy? Show yerself! We want to talk to ya, nothing more!" Jack declares.

There is no reply. A sense of prognosticate dread, lingering from his nightmares, seizes him.

Behind Jack, Flynn Branagáin and the other men from Uath mound whisper to one another, wondering what has become of Emmy. They stand ready, looking and watching for anything out of the ordinary. The secrets they seek to reveal are hidden from them and the late morning sun.

Jack walks inside the cottage, parting the hanging flotsam with the tip of his long sword. A portion of the common area is cleaner than the rest of the residence. Jack can see a giant pentagram painted on the floor. It's accompanied by a variety of ritual items, all sinister in appearance. Each step brings him closer to a revelation he anticipates, but he is not prepared for the outcome.

No sane man could be.

"Emmy? Where ya be?" Jack queries, moving deeper into the rancid bowels of the cottage, "we know you were only speaking with my wife and daughters not too long ago," he comes to the cauldron and steps on broken bits of pottery. The pieces cover the floor, "your stew is boiling, you couldn't have gone very far," Jack finds a large spoon sitting next to the cauldron. Why not, he tells himself, and fills the ladle with a bit of the broth and sips it and sighs. He takes a breath and continues his banter, "there's no need to-"

Something surfaces in the bubbling roil of vegetables and meat, stopping Jack's banter.

It's a face. It's not a swine's face, as one might assume would be used in a pork stew. No, this face is something else altogether, and not an ingredient you would expect to find. At least in any recipe to be consumed by civilized persons. It takes a moment for his mind to make sense of the distorted, misshapen features, boiled off the bones of the skull.

Fluttering eyelids open, revealing empty slits above a flattened nose. The man's heart skips multiple beats as his mind comprehends what he sees. The lips move with the bubbling brew, spitting out each silent word.

I'm not afraid, Daddy.

Jack spits out the remaining broth in his mouth and drops the spoon and his sword. Bile rises in Jack Mac Tíre's throat as a wave of disgust courses through his being.

"No!" A bellowing roar of grief lets loose from his lungs, followed by a stream of vomit evacuating the contents of his stomach. Offal filled with bits of masticated and partially digested vegetable matter and meat covers the floor of Emmy's cottage. He heaves until there is nothing left, still then his diaphragm continues to convulse and his heart races.

He sees before him the monster of his nightmare, taunting him with a single, yellow eye. Rage fills the voids within Sean Chulainn Mac Tíre. It tears through his body, seizing the man until the man isn't a man anymore.

•

A rumble grows from inside Emmy's cottage. The building shakes on its foundation, the thatching in the roof ripples. Flynn Branagáin sees this and grips his sword with two hands, prepared for the worst.

"The witch got Jack, he was a fool to go in there alone," Fergus says.

"She's no witch. She's a wolfcoat," Ronan adds.

"Wolfcoat?" Fergus raises a curious eyebrow.

"Aye, a legend from the highlands. Evil ones who steal the skins of wolves," Ronan's tone grows colder with each spoken word, "and carry out nefarious deeds in the name of their dark masters."

"That explains the eye, no?" Fergus concludes.

"That it does," Cillian nods. The Walshes agree with grumbles.

"Is this all ya got time to do? Gossip about superstitions like children at a campfire?" Flynn interjects, silencing his companions. Or *what* is *the worst?* He further ponders, keeping his mouth shut, *witches and shape shifting demons? Or Jack being dead?* Flynn assures himself and makes a promise this won't happen while he stands watch. The hope of his promise fades before it can grow.

A giant, hairy *something* bursts through the thatching of the roof, bringing forth an explosion of twigs and sod. Whatever it is, the creature's speed is blinding. Before they can identify it, the monster charges into the men.

A forearm, covered in thick, black fur, smacks Flynn in his face. The blow sends him to the road and knocks him out, cold. His claymore falls to the wayside, out of the reach of the men still standing.

The creature grabs Fergus with its massive hands, knocking the pick out of his hands. The miller struggles and screams in the monster's grasp. It opens the mouth on its canid head, and bites Fergus in the throat. The jaws, lined with razor sharp teeth, snap together and pinch McSweeney's noggin off.

His head flies through the air, eyes and mouth agape, and lands next to Flynn's unconscious body. A fountain of blood pumps from the stump on Fergus' neck. The beast casts the dead body aside and charges into its next intended victim, Donnachadh Walsh.

His father steps in front of him, swinging his sledgehammer. The blow strikes the thing in the face, bringing a whimper and nothing more. Ronan pulls the hammer back to swing again, but the thing knows better. It grabs the senior Walsh by the shoulder.

From behind, Cillian thrusts his pitchfork at the beast. The tines stick into the creature's flesh. He pulls the pitchfork back and stabs the monster on repeat. Streams of brackish blood spit out of the holes, then trickle to nothing as they seal on their own.

The monster ignores the attack.

It's too busy ripping Ronan Walsh's muscular arm from the socket.

Cillian backsteps and trips over Flynn. He drops the pitchfork, tumbling into the ditch between the road and the cornfield. He strikes his head on a rock. It doesn't kill him, but he's knocked out.

The weight of the sledgehammer pulls the dismembered man back, bending his back at the waist. Blood pours down his side, pouring from his shoulder wound. The blacksmith opens his mouth to screech at the shock and pain.

The monster shoves the ball of the humerus bone protruding from Ronan's estranged arm into his mouth, muting him. The force of the strike snaps his head back, breaking his neck before he can die of asphyxiation or blood loss.

Bent at the elbow, Ronan's arm rises out of his mouth and waves at his son before his body collapses to the road. Donny Walsh is treated to a full-frontal view of the man beast.

It snarls at the young man. He pisses himself, drops his own hammer, turns and runs.

It waits until Donnachadh is a fair distance away before it leaps at the teenager. It covers the space with ease. The thing lands on his back, snapping his spine and driving his face into the road. The blow kills him on impact.

The thing kicks back one of its legs, digging the

clawed toes into Donny's ass cheeks. It steps forward holding down the teenager's torso with the lead foot and pushes away with the other.

The boy's legs fly off in opposite directions, each leaving a pink contrail and crimson streak behind it. They land in the ditches on either side of the road, while the creature leaps away.

Toward the Branagáin farm and the Mound.

•

Peggy and her daughters rest on the porch of the Branagáin farm, waiting for the hunting party to return. Moira, the Branagáin matriarch and Myrddyn of Uath Mound, sits with them, talking to the pre-teens. A silver tray of brownies rests on a small table. The girl's lips are smeared with chocolate.

"You are certain Emmy's eye didn't look right?" Moira asks the girls.

"It were gone, mostly. I think it were growing back. I told mum Emmy's a Digger Do, but she wouldn't listen to me," Erin says.

"You did not, I did! I said she's a Digger Do first," Rosie counters, crossing her arms and pouting. Moira says nothing, she only listens.

"No, I said it first," Erin insists. Moira and Peggy laugh, too.

"Well, it doesn't matter," Rosie concedes, "cos I

saw her eye first."

"You did not! I-"

A screeching cry ends the argument between the siblings. They stop and cock their heads to the sound. The banshee wail turns the adults' jovial smiles into concerned frowns, and they too look for its origin.

"Mum, I don't feel well," Erin says, holding her belly.

From outside they can hear the cattle are spooked by it. The ungulates moo and trot about in circles. The baying of hounds joins in the chorus, growing louder as the dogs come closer to the farm. It builds into a chaotic frenzy of barks and growls. Rosie cries, but not from the dogs.

"I'm going to be sick, I need to go to the outhouse," the young girl says between her tears, she tugs on her mother's shawl, "mum, please."

"Okay, let's go," Peggy tells her daughter before turning to Moira, "what's the problem with the hounds?"

"The men, the dogs were with them, you'd think they'd stop them from fighting," Moira says. Peggy nods and sighs, wondering what could be causing the dogs to fight.

"Aye," Peggy answers, "well, the girls need to go use the outhouse, and to be honest, so do I. My belly is off from something I ate. Let's see what the fuss is all about, shall we? Come, girls," she points to her daughters and coaxes them to join her with a finger.

The barking dogs stop without so much as a whimper, as if obeying the Mac Tíre matron's command.

It's about time, Peggy keeps to herself. The girls go to their mother and follow the women from the enclosed porch. Moira leads the way and opens the door. She steps down the stairs, out of the threshold to learn something is waiting for them outside.

Moira Branagáin walks face first into it.

It takes Peggy a moment to see the attacker. A long, sinewed arm, covered in coarse black hairs, stretches out, the rest of the body obscured by the house. A clawed hand has Moira's head in a death grip. She struggles and punches at the arm, but nothing happens. Her legs slip out from underneath her and the hand clenches Moira's head, holding her aloft.

Blood seeps out from the claws and trickles down the woman's face. Moira Branagáin screams in agony, frantically trying to escape. The fingers holding her clench further and crack bone. Droplets of blood scatter about, decorating the walls. The woman's shrieking intensifies in volume and pitch until her voice cracks and her body goes limp.

Peggy can do nothing but stand on the porch. Moira's thrashing body prevents the Mac Tíre matron from helping her friend. The children, their eyes already wide with fear, scream in horror. Peggy Mac Tíre pulls them close to her as the thing releases Moira to gravity's whims. The Branagáin matriarch falls onto the stairs, limp.

Outside the farmhouse, the mangled bodies of the Branagáin's wolfhounds lay in a pile of wet meat and bones. Inside, a pool of blood spreads out and surrounds Moira's body.

Something hairy, part beast and part human, steps into the puddle and blocks their exit. It stands over Moira's body and stares at the Mac Tíres. One of the thing's amber eyes hangs from its socket by a thread of nerves and blood vessels, the other remains set deep into a massive canine head.

Peggy and the girls step back, away from the creature. She smells something horrible, like rotten eggs, and looks down. Puddles of liquid shit are forming around her daughters' feet, dripping down their legs. She pushes the girls behind her, doing her best to hold her own bowels.

The creature opens its gigantic maw, snaggle toothed with wicked fangs ...

And howls.

7

Emmy O'Sullivan sits at the table in her dining area, waiting. She knows they'll come for her, sooner than later. She knows they'll blame her. Why not? They already call her a witch, and they're justified in doing so. She's not innocent, by any stretch of the imagination. She did all of this for the blood of her love.

An Mac Tíre mo ghrá.

When you play with the darkness, it always turns back on you. She did her part, as the god told her, in the heat of lust, on *His* day.

"Do as I bid, and ye shall be close with thy love for as long as you both shall live," the god said to her.

Emmy did it all in accordance with the ritual, yet still, they will come. What is she to do? The curse will soon take over her love, bringing him to her. She need only wait.

The god provides.

The *luchthonn* came to her on the night's wind, presented to her by the god. She donned the beast's shirt and went wolfing on the god's night. She took what was rightfully hers to take.

Now her head throbs in pain, the epicenter radiates from her left eye. It struggles to heal, a result of the iron in Jack's tomahawk.

She hears them approaching, the harlot and her spawn. They speak ill of her, out of earshot, but Emmy knows. She has eyes above, and ears below. The crows, flying through the clouds, see for her. The worms, blind as they burrow in the earth, hear the words resonate through the soil.

Emmy's a Digger Do... the girls say, not realizing how close to many truths they are. The *Dearg Due* are *neamh-mairbh* and Emmy O'Sullivan is very much alive.

For the time being.

Their mum, Emmy knows, is another story.

She be a changeling, thirsty for the blood of kings, Emmy recalls, *I was there, when the midwife took a red-haired baby from Goody Crouch.*

Emmy waits for Goody Mac Tire to knock on the door before moving from her bench, after all, she doesn't want the *fae* harlot to know she's been waiting. Emmy sees through Goody Mac Tire's facade. She knows her to be *leannán sídhe.*

She pulls her shawl over her head to obscure the wound. Emmy's skin itches. She can feel the wolf's coat underneath, wanting to burst through.

It knows a fight is coming.

She holds it back and opens the door. Peggy Mac Tíre stands in the doorway, her daughters holding the empty crocks, once filled with stew. She'd love nothing more than to bury her snout in the *sídhe*'s belly and rip her guts out.

But the god forbids it.

She greets Goody Mac Tíre, assuming this won't end well. Emmy isn't caught off guard by the harlot's kindness. She knows it to be a ruse. She sees the pentacles around the girls' necks and knows Goody Mac Tíre's intent is to taunt her. But the revelation of a family feast?

They all ate it? This will be interesting.

Emmy secures the crocks from the girls. Both little shits are staring at her. She knows they can see her wound, and it pleases her to the point of jubilation, and closes the door with her foot before the children can say anything.

She listens for them to leave, then throws the crocks at the hearth. The pottery strikes the cauldron and smashes into pieces, scattered about on the floor. Her eye shifts in hue, from hazel to amber. She tears her dress and tunic off, casting the clothing aside, exposing herself.

The wolf takes over.

The woman falls to the floor inside the pentagram, convulsing and thrashing on the floor. Rivulets of blood cover her as she shifts. Her body twitches, her skin stings, as a thousand,

No-hundreds of thousands-

needles poke through. Thick, black hairs, slicked in blood rise. The hairs grow across her body. Her chest tightens and narrows, her breasts flatten and stretch with the ribs. Bones snap and crackle as if someone were popping corn. Her belly constricts and tightens around her hips.

She pushes up on her hands and knees, her back arching. Her legs break and heal, and break and heal, over and over. Her knees drop and the ankle of each foot stretches out. A tail grows, vertebrae by vertebrae, protruding from her ass, a bush of fur blooming from it.

On her forequarters, Emmy's arms are faring about as well as her legs. The bones break and shift and heal in turn and her elbows turn in. Her thumb pulls up the side of her arm while the nails on her fingertips grow thicker and longer.

The head always shifts last. Emmy's nasal cavity and jaw stretch out, dripping fluids off her flesh. Long fangs grow, protruding from her newly formed snout.

Her field of vision narrows. Her visual spectrum is limited, but her aural and olfactory senses are enhanced. Canine ears can hear the men outside her cottage. She smells their fear as millions of scent cells grow on her nose.

"Emmy?" she hears the voice and her heart stops. A loud rapping follows. Emmy knows who it is.

An Mac Tíre mo ghrá.

Her love.

Knowing she cannot face her love like this, the time has come to leave. He's seen her go wolfing before, and his gift was an iron axe.

The wolf howls. It's a lonely, baleful howl. When it waxes, she slips out the back of the cottage, and into the wood line, hidden from the eyes of the hunters. It darts across the road, the men are too busy watching the cottage's door, and into the cornfield. Her destination isn't far away.

·

The men from Uath mound lay strewn about on the road next to the collapsed wreckage of Emmy O'Sullivan's cottage. They are reflections, in a sense, of one another; each felled by the witch's curses.

The taste of copper and dirt stirs Flynn Branagáin. The ground is stiff and his body aches. His eyes open, revealing a nightmare of carnage. A pit grows in his belly. Flynn sits up, pushing himself out of the blood puddle with both hands. And not simply anyone's blood, either.

It's Fergus' blood.

At least he assumes the headless corpse wearing his clothing belongs to Fergus McSweeney. He can identify the upper half of young Donnachadh, and wonders where the bottom half ran off to. But most of all, he puzzles over Ronan's urge to eat his own arm.

Where is the thing that attacked us? Where are Jack and Cillian? Flynn wonders. *Did it take them?* He stands, then retrieves his claymore, and wipes the blood off the steel blade. He surveys the damage. At least three dead. The cottage's roof fell in, and a portion of a wall tipped over. The remaining three are teetering on borrowed time.

"Jack? Cillian? Emmy?" Flynn proclaims. No one answers. He jogs down the embankment to the house, "Jack? Emmy?" The results are the same. The door is still open, jammed in place by clumps of sod from the thatch.

Something catches Flynn's eye on the floor. His heart jumps in anticipation of discovering his friend. But it's only his sword, Wolf Cleaver. The creaking walls give Flynn pause, before he slides in the door and pulls the sword back, snagging the pommel with his foot.

"Flynn!" Cillian Kelley shouts from the road. A relieved Flynn retrieves Jack's blade and spins around to see the other survivor. Blood covers Clillian's face, but he's alive.

"Cillian! Thank the god yer alive. You look like shite!" Flynn hurries back to the road, eager to get away from the cottage.

"Yer never one to hang an ass, are ya Branagáin?"

"The god provides," Flynn crosses himself.

"Aye. Did ya find Jack?" Cillian asks.

"Nay. I found his sword though."

"Emmy's bewitched him, for sure."

"We don't know about that. What we should do is go back to the mound and talk to the Myrddyn. She's back there with Jack's kin. She'll tell us what to do, and know who we should be calling a witch," Cillian nods, agreeing with his friend's proposal. Flynn hands Wolf Cleaver to Cillian, and the pair run down the road, back to the Branagáin farm and Uath Mound.

Halfway there, they hear the howling. It sends chills up their spines.

"Mayhaps we should take the corn? It will provide cover if the beast is at the farm," Cillian suggests. Flynn nods, and the duo bounds off into the rows of corn.

When they near the farm, the men slow their pace, using the vegetation to their advantage. Upon their arrival, a scene of carnage reveals itself between the stalks of corn. Littering the road, they see the remains of the mangled dogs, or at least what is left of them, first.

What follows is the stuff of nightmares.

8

The wolf watches the property from the safety of corn, obscured from detection by the tall stalks.

And waits.

The farmhouse and barn stand between the wolf and the hunting dogs. Before long, a mournful, agonizing howl from down the holler sends the hounds into a barking frenzy. The wolf fights the urge to respond in kind.

Soon the dogs focus their attention on a single, black shadow. They lunge at darkness, their teeth gnashing, their jaws snapping. The shadow swipes them away with the ambivalence of a beast of burden's tail shooing flies. The animals whimper before being torn apart.

The shadow leaps, casting its darkness across the farmhouse. The wolf cannot see it.

But the wolf can hear the creature's baneful

howl. The lamenting cry is joined by another, then two more, each raising in pitch and building to a shrill crescendo.

Satisfied, the wolf retreats deeper into the corn and hides.

It is not alone.

•

Flynn Branagáin and Cillian Kelley skulk through the corn rows, watching for the monster. The swords in their hands are ready to cleave anything, man or beast, they encounter. High above, flocks of black birds swarm in patterns, creating spiral patterns in the air. Turkey vultures circle on the higher, warmer currents.

Waiting to feed.

Flynn sees his wife's body lying in a clump on the steps of the porch. The howling of a wolf pack sends shivers up the men's spines. The duck back into the foliage, hoping they can't see the monsters...

The monsters won't see them.

Flynn and Cillian turn to each other, terror on their faces.

"A pack? Are you fecking kidding me?" Flynn whispers. Cillian shakes his head, throws a finger up to his lips, points one finger up, then indicates something is behind Flynn. The Branagáin patriarch furrows his brow, wondering what Cillian is up to, before he looks down the rows and sees it, laying in the dirt between rows of corn.

A wolf's tail.

•

The wolf's ears perk, twisting to the sides. There is movement in the corn and in the sky. Looking up with one good eye, a maddening torrent of flapping black wings, cut through the air. To the aft and fore, the scent of corn blinds the wolf to all others. But the sound of moving cornstalks is unmistakable.

A grunt precedes reaped corn stalks, husks, and leaves falling about. The wolf takes a moment too long in its decision to bolt. A din of steel resonates as a sword blade sticks into the ground, blocking the way.

The wolf spins around, and leaps through the stalks, landing in a clear patch.

And wishes it hadn't.

•

Chaos ensues as Flynn swings his claymore, cutting through the corn stalks, blazing a path the wolf won't be able to hide under. Cillian takes up the rear, waiting in the clearing, Jack's claymore held at the ready with both of his hands.

Distracted by their quarry, neither man hears the corn behind them moving as something charges through the stalks.

Cillian, standing alone in the clearing, doesn't see the man-wolf creature, a single eye dangling from its eye socket, burst through the wall of plants with muscular arms. They grab Mr. Kelley by the shoulders, pulling him back into the corn. The sword flies from his hands and lands on the ground.

Flynn stabs his sword into the earth, blocking the wolf's path. It spins around and leaps away.

"Feck!" Branagáin curses, and pulls the blade free of the dirt, spinning on his heels and launching after the wolf.

Blood rains down on the clearing, covering Flynn in crimson. A wet thud and splash of bloody mud catches his attention on the ground.

Cillian Kelley's head, the features frozen in a death mask of surprise, stares back at him with dead eyes.

The wolf lands at Flynn's feet, its snout inches from Cillian's face, and yelps in fear. The animal pushes back with its hindlegs and trips Flynn. He lands on his shoulder, the Branagáin family claymore, *Solais*.

He's not sure if the coppery taste in his mouth

is his blood, or Cillian's. When he sees what killed Cillian, Flynn stops giving a shit about who's blood is whose.

Hovering over him with its massive arms raised to strike, is the man-wolf thing from Emmy's cottage, its eye still dangling out of the socket.

It's not alone.

Next to it is a female, covered in coarse black hair. Behind them are two more, albeit a portion of the size of the others. It doesn't make them any less terrifying, with razor pointed teeth in their snouted mouths.

The wolf is lying next to him, shaking. The animal's tail is lodged between its legs, ears laid back in submission.

It fears something more than me? Flynn wonders. He jumps to his feet, sees Wolf Cleaver is within reach, and grabs the sword. He stands ready to strike back when a storm of black birds swarms down into the clearing.

The creatures rear back as hundreds of crows and swallows form a vortex. Flynn swings the claymore wildly, batting birds away in the process. Feathers and blood fill the air.

Then it stops. The birds fly away into the sky, as thunderheads grow and blot out the sun, casting a shadow of darkness on the field. Down filters to the ground and the chaos subsides. The dark shadow forms a line between Flynn and the wolf, and the wolf-things.

Flynn stands, defiant, with Wolf Cleaver at the ready. The wolf cowers behind his legs, its skin bubbling and shifting, the hair falling off its skin.

It's changing? What witchcraft is this? Flynn moves away from it and stops. A bolt of lightning strikes in on the top of Morgan Hill, and thunder rolls down its slopes. The wolf-things snarl and menace even as they, too, shift back into their natural forms, the largest one's left eye dangling swinging.

Underneath the clamor a hissing, clicking sound slithers and grows, chittering through the rows of corn.

Above the tops of the tallest plants, a figure rises, elevated by a preternatural force. To Flynn Branagáin's shock, it's his wife, Moira, Myrddyn of the Uath Mound.

Mostly.

What's become of my bride? Flynn wonders to himself, unsure how she can walk, let alone hover in the air before them.

Moira sways in the sky, the winds holding her aloft, the folds of her dress waving in the breeze. The right half of Moira's head is caved in at the forehead, and she's missing an eye. A blue goo drips from the wound at her temple, trailing down her cheek, staining it. Her mouth opens with a crack, the jaw is unaligned.

Her head cocks to the left, and to the right, and a snap follows, resetting the bones and ligaments. She speaks. The words are unnatural, and not in Moira's typical cadence. They're forced, as if the matriarch spoke with another person's mouth.

"*Soláthraíonn an Dia.*"

The god provides.

9

Dusk falls on the foothills. On the Branagáin farm, a dozen standing stones encircle a mound, at its center is a well. Emmy O'Sullivan is tied to one of these stones. The crows circle above, watching and waiting to see what unfolds below.

Haggard and still missing an eye, Emmy knows the carrion eaters will not feed on her this day. She does not fear what is to come. She does not weep, or tremble. She is, instead, relieved. The stress of this affair has taken its toll on the woman.

Now she wants to rest.

The thing which was once Moira Branagáin hovers, her arms outstretched, before the *Well of the God* on Uath Mound. The wraith's head is covered by a black shawl, but Emmy knows what lies beneath its fabric. She knows what watches her through Moira's remaining eye.

The god provides ...

The Mac Tíre brood approaches the mound. Skyclad, their skin is painted with woad spirals. They carry a small, pine box, a family member at each corner of the rectangular-

Casket, Emmy notes to herself, *it's a casket for me.*

Behind them, his face covered by the bronzed wolf mask of the clan Cathain, walks Flynn Branagáin. He holds *Solais* in his hands, its blade pointed at the family. The faithful of Uath Mound follow, wearing linen robes and yellow wreaths of Mountain Ash. Flynn and Moira's daughter, Gruoch, leads the cortege. The Van Bramers, the Dutch cobblers who first settled in Tinker's Falls. The Mac Boedhes, the tanner, and the Finlays, who work the mills. The widows, sons and daughters of the McSweeneys, the Kelleys, and the Walshes. And finally, the keening sisters, Léanmhar and Siobhán O' Riordan, breathing their lamenting melodies.

The procession stops in front of Moira, and places the coffin on the ground, the foot facing Emmy. Goody Mac Tíre opens the box and holds the lid aside. Jack Mac Tíre and Flynn Branagáin stand to either side of Emmy, never once looking at her face.

"Ye can't look at me, can ye, you weak minded dogs. Yer blinded by the harlot's *fae* magic," she curses at them.

"Éimhear Ní Súilleabháin" the Myrddyn declares, her words surrounded by clicks and hisses, "ya stand accused of murder most foul, before the eye of the god of the mound. What have ya to say?"

"I be guilty as charged," Emmy replies. There's no use in lying. The wraith-like thing, which was once Moira Branagáin points at Emmy, then at the box.

"*Soláthraíonn an dia,*" the Myrddyn says.

"*The god provides,*" the faithful say in unison.

The men hold Emmy against the rock and untie her. She feels a moment of relief as the bonds lose their grip and circulation returns to her limbs.

It's short lived.

The men lift Emmy away from the standing stone. Caught off guard, she thrashes and wiggles, but is unable to free herself from their grasp. She calls the wolf, but the fear of iron keeps it at bay.

Emmy is not surprised when they force her into the confines of the coffin. They dislocate a shoulder and a foot bent backwards, cramps. But it's nothing in comparison to agony to come.

Jack breaks both of her legs in the process of fitting her into the coffer. They snap with ease. A shrill scream pours from her lungs as her shins crack, and the broken bones rip through the skin.

The wolf urges her to flee, to take over, but it cannot. Then Emmy understands why. The box isn't pine. It is Mountain Ash.

Witchwood.

She fights back, and lunges forward, managing to grip the edge of the box with her fingers. It's a mistake. Jack takes the casket cover from his wife and swings it at Emmy's head. The two-inch-thick board connects, knocking her silly, and back into the confines of the box.

Jack reaches in and holds Emmy's head in place. The wolf wants to fight. Her features bubble, black hairs stick up through her skin, only to retreat a moment later. Peggy kneels and grabs hold of Emmy's tongue. Flynn steps forward with the claymore, and with a flick of the blade's tip, he cuts Emmy's tongue from her mouth.

She screeches in agony, thrashing within the confinement of the box. Jack Mac Tire Holds her jaw firm, as Peggy stuffs Emmy's mouth with a handful of herbs. Peggy Mac Tire does nothing to hide her smile.

The twinkle of the fae shimmers in her eyes. It's the last thing Emmy sees before Jack slams the lid down, breaking all the fingers in Emmy's hands, and extinguishing the light.

Inside the box, within the void of darkness,

Emmy O'Sullivan weeps. She knows where they are taking her, she can feel the power of the *fae* grow with each step her pall bearers take.

Outside the box, a banshee's wail lingers along the trail in their wake. The keeners harmonize with her cries.

•

At the center of an orchard of Mountain Ash and apple trees, near Uath Mound, are the Mac Tíres' standing stones. Triskelion swirls, etched into the face of the bedrock, adorn the slabs of bedrock, but tonight's visitors can't see them. Around them grows a bed of majestic sunflowers. The plants stand taller than the stones, obscuring the monoliths from sight.

Underneath the gaze of the gigantic flowers, a pentagram of chalk encircles a clearing. At its epicenter is a small grave, dug earlier in the day, waiting to be filled. The faithful of Uath Mound gather around the edge of the circle in silence as the McEntire family sets the coffin carrying Emmy O'Sullivan into the grave. She struggles and screams from within its confines.

Flynn Branagáin takes his place next to his wife, or at least used to be. The former Moira Branagáin, still playing the role of the Myrddyn, steps forward. Her face still covered by a shawl, the

Bandrúi raises her hands above her head. It is a cue to the faithful of Uath Mound to depart.

They step forward, one by one, each scooping a shovel of earth from the pile, and drops it on Emmy's prison. At first the falling dirt covers the casket, then it muffles Emmy's vain struggles, until the last of the grave is filled in by Jack Mac Tíre.

Peggy stands next to him, Erin and Rose in tow. She sings as he finishes burying Emmy alive. It's a lamenting song, of loves lost, and found. The keeners lend the melody, wailing in key.

> *"An Mac Tíre mo ghrá.*
> *An Badhbh- Bronntanas na beatha*
> *An Badhbh- An Scriosóir*
> *An t-anam Badhbh-Éillithe*
> *An Badhbh- Cuirim fáilte romhat abhaile*
> *An Mac Tíre mo ghrá."*

Six feet below, not quite living, and most certainly far from dead, Emmy can hear Goody Mac Tíre sing the words of her fae-bound spell. Emmy frets not. Peggy can think she's won for now.

The god has provided Emmy O'Sullivan all of eternity to plan her revenge.

ST ROOSTER BOOKS

ST ROOSTER BOOKS

ACKNOWLEDGMENTS

This novella shouldn't have happened. Last October, Garrett Cook prompted me to write a monster story for a Halloween horror story workshop. What started as an attempt to re-invent the Wolf Man trope ended up becoming much more. The 3,000-word assignment grew into a 10,000-word novelette. My mentor at Stitched Smile Publications, Lisa Vasquez, reviewed the story as part of another proposed collection. She lost her shit, advising me to turn the story into a standalone book.

And then author and publisher Tim Murr mentioned how much he loved Stephen King's Cycle of the Werewolf. By the time I finished the contents, my goal changed, much like the shapeshifting gods of old.

I love werewolves. *The Wolf Man* is one of my favorite horror films. *The Howling, An American Werewolf in London, Dog Soldiers*, and *Ginger Snaps* top the pile. *Werewolf the Apocalypse* was my *World of Darkness* choice, Vampire came second. SP Somtow's *Moondance*. Nancy A. Collins' *Walking Wolf* and *Wild Blood*. *The Wolf's Hour* by Robert

McCammon. Skip & Spector's *Animals*. These books have thrilled me for decades.

Then, a few years ago, I read *MONGRELS* by Stephen Graham Jones. It's a fantastic read and got me thinking. The rich mythology Jones developed for his werewolf book, the manners in which he flipped the trope on its head, and what he added to the genre.

So, I wrote *Fireflies and Apple Pies* and the rest snowballed from it. I created a vibrant setting for the stories in apple country, upstate New York, a region whose rolling hills are reminiscent of Eire. I created a secret society of neo-pagans, and breathed life into them by delving deep into pre-Christianity Gaelic, Celtic, and Pict mythology. I started mining books, like Adam Neville's *The Ritual*, for examples of how to address the manners in which the faithful worship their cosmic entity.

None is more famous in the old Irish myths than Cu Cullhain. His exploits are the stuff of legend, and share aspects with Hellenic heroes, demi-Gods and deities. I took liberties with the old myths, shifting events around to make a more cohesive narrative. The result is an exercise in folk horror, telling a cautionary tale about the dangers of infidelity.

I'd like to thank the witches and werewolves who helped this novella come together. This is the result of forcing myself to write by paying for monthly workshops and honing my craft. Garrett Cook is a fucking genius and if you have the opportunity to take a class from this man, do yourself a favor and take it. Then there are my beta readers on this project: Meghan Rose Daniels, Amy Baker, and Jewel Tiffany. Plus, my podcasting brothers who lent their eyes and editing skills to the stories collected here: Scott Groverston, Walter Ball, and Skip Novak. All the blurb readers and other peers who gave me advice and suggestions, like Patrick Freivald and John, err, Todd Keisling. Thanks, again, to Tim Murr for humoring me by reading the first story and suggesting the final project you see before you. Stephanie Murr, Tim's partner in crime and an excellent illustrator, who brought some of the more iconic scenes in the stories to life. And a big, huge shout out to cover artist Lynne Hansen, who found a way to go get me to change the title. She's an outstanding person and made the words you read look like a million bucks with her cover art.

It's poetic to save the best for last, right? So, without further delay, a huge thank you to Matt Byers - Dude! Bro! (fist bump) - you truly are the Darque Bard.

Sláinte!
Thomas R Clark 5/13/21

ST ROOSTER BOOKS

ABOUT THE AUTHOR

Thomas R Clark is a musician, writer, and podcast producer & engineer. He is the author of the 2021 Splatterpunk Award Nominated BELLA'S BOYS, GOOD BOY, and THE DEATH LIST—published through Stitched Smile Publications, and THE GOD PROVIDES, from St. Rooster Books. His journalism has appeared in Memento Mori Ink, Rue Morgue, This Is Infamous, and House of Stitched Magazine. Tom lives in Central New York with his wife and their canine companions.

ST ROOSTER BOOKS

ST ROOSTER BOOKS

Also Available from St Rooster Books

From Tim Murr;

The Gray Man

978-1799252177

Lose This Skin; Collected Short Works 1994-2011

978-1530351633

Conspiracy of Birds/Hounds of Doom

978-1516920631

City Long Suffering

978-1519588074

Motel on Fire; Stories

978-1543039016

Neon Sabbath; Stories

978-1721039708

My Skull is Full of Black Smoke; Stories

979-8680276099

Collection/Various Authors

ST ROOSTER BOOKS

To Be One with You; An Anthology of Parasitic Horror 2018 featuring Paul Kane, Marie O'Regan, Jeffery X Martin, Peter Oliver Wonder, Adam Millard, DJ Tyrer, David W Barbee, Ross Peterson
978-1724516787

Kids of the Black Hole; A Punksploitation Anthology featuring Sarah Miner, Chris Hallock, Paul Lubaczewski, and Jeremy Lowe
978-1072962724

The Blind Dead Ride Out of Hell; A Literary Tribute to the Amando de Ossorio Films featuring Sam Richard, Heather Drain, Paul Lubaczewski, Mark Zirbel, Jeremy Lowe, and Jerome Reuter
979-8692365187

A New Life by Paul Lubaczewski
979-8615384066

Blood & Mud by John Baltisberger

The God Provides by Thomas R Clark
979-8520227076

3 Hits from the Holler by Paul Lubaczewski
979-8707581984

Abhorrent Siren by John Baltisberger
978-1955745024

Let the World Drown: An Anthology of Sea Horror featuring Brian M Sammons, Lee Franklin, Jedediah

ST ROOSTER BOOKS

Smith, AK McCarthy, Anthony S Buoni, BE Goose, Paul Lubaczewski, Jeremy Lowe, John Baltisberger, and Carter Johnson
979-8739852915

ST ROOSTER BOOKS